They were coming back . . .

The men rode into view, galloping along the trail two abreast.

Long Rider cocked his rifle. Then they were all reaching for their rifles. Long Rider saw his chance. He raised the Sharps and aimed . . . straight at the saddlebags of the man who had the dynamite.

Long Rider fired. The heavy slug slammed straight into the saddlebags, knocking the man's horse sideways. The dynamite went off with a thunderous roar. Horses and men were blown to pieces, but Long Rider saw that only one of the men who'd come hunting for him was still alive, a wreck of a man lying on the ground, missing one arm, his face in shreds. He heard Long Rider approach, and looked up, out of his single remaining eye. He croaked something from a ruined throat. Perhaps it was a plea.

Long Rider shot him through the heart. The man fell back, dead.

Then Long Rider turned away from the carnage and urged his horse down the trail, pressing him forward, as quickly as the big black could go. . . .

Also in the LONG RIDER Series

LONG RIDER

VENGEANCE TOWN

CLAY DAWSON

13

CHARTER/DIAMOND BOOKS, NEW YORK

VENGEANCE TOWN

A Charter/Diamond Book/published by arrangement
with the author

PRINTING HISTORY
Charter/Diamond edition/December 1990

ISBN: 1-55773-428-3

Charter/Diamond Books are published by The Berkley Publishing
Group, 200 Madison Avenue, New York, New York 10016.
The name "CHARTER/DIAMOND" and its logo are trademarks
belonging to Charter Communications, Inc.

PRINTED IN THE UNITED STATES OF AMERICA

10 9 8 7 6 5 4 3 2 1

VENGEANCE
TOWN

CHAPTER ONE

The land was arid, as was most of the land in this particular corner of the Arizona high country. However, a little rain fell from time to time, trapped by the mountains to the east. Green showed, a light, pleasing green. Hardy plants satisfied themselves from the occasional summer showers. The clean sandy ground was spotted with mesquite, chaparral, short, tough grasses, and occasional cactus. The flat places were bordered by rimrock, which rose straight up from the valley floors, layer upon colored layer, cut into strange shapes by wind and rain. It was an easy land to look at, even beautiful. But not an easy land to live in. There was no softness.

A horseman rode slowly across the floor of one of the more level valleys, heading west. He had come down from the pine-clad mountains, which now lay twenty miles behind him. He was a tall man on a tall horse, riding easily, the way a man rides when he has been on a horse all of his life. He wore an old slouch hat, faded and stained with age. A long linen duster covered unremarkable clothes, but the duster was open far enough to show the butt of a pistol protruding, butt forward, cavalry style, on his right hip. Instead of riding boots, he wore a pair of soft, well-oiled moccasins. He was not a man to attract immediate attention—except for the unusual paleness of his eyes, which were set in a lean face, eyes that seemed even more pale because of his tan, that dark mahogany color that comes from a lifetime of exposing fair skin to the sun. Long, sandy-colored hair, showing streaks of sun bleaching, hung down over his shoulders. The clothing might look ordinary enough, but not the man.

His name was a matter of conjecture, depending on which world he found himself in. When he was in the white man's world, he called himself Gabe. He'd been in the white man's world for some time now. Too damned long. But by now there was very little left except the white man's world.

Gabe liked the land he was riding through. It was almost as flat as, but more broken up than, his native land, the Dakota plains, through which he had ridden as a boy. Ridden with the People, not realizing that they were not the only people—until it was too late, until their time of mastery over the land had been taken from them, taken in blood and starvation.

He liked the cleanness of this land. The soil was heavy, sandy, it did not kick up in little puffs of dust as his horse passed over it. Although he had been riding all day, he did not feel particularly dirty. The temperature was warm, although not blazing hot, but he was not sweaty; the dry, clean breeze evaporated his sweat before it could stick to him. Still, he was tired. And thirsty. His water bottle was low, and he had not seen running water for some time. He wondered if he would be able to find some low spot, showing more green than elsewhere, then dig for water. The trouble was, despite the flatness of the land, it was difficult to see very far. Thick green bushes, some as large as small trees, bushes with a piny look about them, obscured his view. He'd have to find some place where the ground was a little higher, so that he could see where he was.

The land seemed to rise a little to his right. He turned in that direction. Within a few hundred yards he saw a small ridge ahead. He rode up onto it. Now he was above the scattered bushes, his view cut only by distant tables of rimrock. He scanned the area for thicker, deeper greens that might indicate an underground stream.

None showed immediately. Instead, he saw a town in the distance, about two or three miles away. It took him a moment to decide that it was a town, and not just an ugly, low, grayish geological formation.

Gabe hesitated. He did not like towns, he preferred this open ground. On the other hand, he was still thirsty. And—he made himself face it—he was also a little thirsty for the sound of human voices. When he'd lived with the People, there had always been the sound of voices, the boasting of men, the soft chatter of women, the shriller sounds of children playing, the barking of excited dogs. For many years, for his entire youth, he'd spent most of his time surrounded by a small slice of humanity, his own portion of it, a people who belonged to him, as he belonged to them. But it had not been a town, not a white man's town, with its coldness and inhumanity, its greed and selfishness. The whites were not a people. They were a collection of individuals who strove for advantage over one another. Gabe hated that striving. Still, they were men. He decided to ride on into the town.

He almost changed his mind when he reached the main street. That was pretty much it, one dusty street, bordered by faded, unpainted wooden buildings. A few alleys branched off to the sides, leading toward various houses and shacks. It was not a prepossessing place.

Gabe might have ridden right on through if his thirst had not won out. The biggest building in town was a saloon. He licked his lips, thinking about what was inside. Water might be healthier, but every once in a while . . .

Gabe parked his horse at a hitching rack directly in front of the saloon. He started toward the swinging doors, hesitated, then went back to his horse and removed his rifles from their saddle scabbards. There were two rifles: a lever-action Winchester and a Sharps carbine. He carried them with him, up onto the splintered, dirty boardwalk, then pushed his way in through the swinging doors with the muzzle of the Winchester.

Gabe did not like saloons, but a man had to go to where they had what he wanted. He stood in the doorway for a moment, taking in the interior, instinctively scanning the room for potential unpleasant surprises. The light was fairly dim, but even so, he could see that the place was not very clean. The sawdust that covered the floor was very old, balled up with spat-out tobacco juice. Dust coated anything that had not recently been sat on or used. The place was almost empty; besides the bartender, there were only two other people in the saloon, two men who appeared to be professional drunks. Gabe ignored them.

By now Gabe's thirst was truly monumental. He went over to a table that was situated close to a blank side wall and leaned his rifles against the wall. Then he turned and walked toward the bar.

Gabe began to pay a lot of attention to the bartender. The man had been watching him intently since he'd entered the place. It had not been the usual bored stare of a bartender. As Gabe drew nearer, he sensed a cold calculation in the way the man was watching him approach. Gabe instinctively distrusted him.

However, when Gabe reached the bar, the man's eyes crinkled into a warm, welcoming smile. "Well, stranger," the bartender said. "We don't usually have people pushing their way through the doors with the muzzle of a rifle."

So that was it. The bartender must have been alarmed by the sight of a rifle barrel poking its way in between the swinging doors. "My hands were full," Gabe replied, pleased by the man's friendliness.

"We can put something better in your hands than rifles. Let me fill 'em up with something cool and wet. What'll it be, mister?"

Gabe licked his lips. "Root beer."

The bartender looked at him blankly. "Huh?"

Gabe felt a moment of annoyance. He hated the reaction his request usually provoked. "Root beer," he said, a little more truculently. "You got any?"

The bartender's smile came back. He seemed to be able to turn it on and off at will. "Yeah. I think so. It's just that we don't get a lot of requests for it. Root beer ain't a big seller around these parts."

One of the drunks, seated at a table not far away, snorted in laughter. Gabe slowly turned to face him. One look into those pale, expressionless eyes encouraged the drunk to stop laughing.

Gabe turned back to the bar. The bartender was rummaging around beneath a counter. He pulled out a dusty, dark bottle that had obviously been there for some time. He spent a few seconds wiping the bottle clean, which Gabe appreciated. The bartender put the bottle down on the counter behind the bar and started to open it. He seemed to be having trouble, it took him a long time to get it open, but Gabe could not see what the problem was; the bartender's back was in the way.

The bartender finally turned around with the open bottle and set it on the bar in front of Gabe. He was reaching behind him for a glass when Gabe stopped him. "I like to drink it straight out of the bottle."

The bartender was still smiling. "Each man to his own. That'll be a dime."

Gabe thought that the price was a little high, but then, in this place, root beer was probably an exotic drink. He fished a dime out of his pocket, laid it on the bar, and walked back to his table. As he sat down, he glanced around him casually. Drinking root beer in a saloon was a good way to start a fight. But the two drunks, one of them already having tried laughing, then thinking better of it, were both staring morosely into their drinks.

Gabe raised the bottle to his lips, took a medium-sized sip. His mouth filled with the rich root taste of the drink, the sweetness. This and sarsaparilla were the strongest things he ever drank. He loathed alcohol, not because of any personal dislike for the taste of it, but because he had seen what it had done to his people, how it had turned calm, strong men into murderous idiots. He had seen an entire nation of people ruined by alcohol—seen wives sold for another bottle, lodges and horses traded away, old friends slaughtered in a moment of drunken rage. He had vowed never to touch it.

Instead, he had his root beer and sarsaparilla. And he loved them both. As he slowly sipped from the bottle, he wondered if they had any sarsaparilla. Sometimes they kept it on hand for the ladies, although the few who'd come into a place like this probably weren't what white society liked to call ladies.

Sarsaparilla might be better than this particular brand of root beer. As he drank, he realized that it had a peculiarly bitter aftertaste. Perhaps it had been sitting on the shelf for too long. He thought of complaining, but the bartender was beaming another warm smile in his direction. Why embarrass the man? "You like it?" the bartender asked. "It's made locally."

A local product. They must use some roots not used in other root beers. That might account for the odd aftertaste. Gabe took a big swig, then nodded back into the bartender's smile. That was a mistake. Moving his head made him feel suddenly dizzy. He shook his head. That made it worse. He wondered if the sun had affected him. He hadn't eaten very much today. Maybe all this sugar after a day in the saddle . . .

Bitter. Dizzy. He shook his head again, then looked up. The bartender's smile seemed to be growing wider. Gabe slowly realized that the bartender was now standing a lot closer to him. The man's features blurred; there seemed to be something wrong with Gabe's vision . . . as if he were looking down a long, dark tunnel bordered by bright lights.

Disorientation. Gabe blinked. There was something right in front of him, close to his eyes. It took him several seconds to realize that it was dirty, splintered wood, and filthy sawdust. The floor! He was lying on the floor!

What the hell was happening? Gabe felt someone rolling him over. He did not seem to be able to help, his body was incapable of movement. He saw the bartender's smile again, quite close to his face, looking down at him, but this time the smile was cold, gloating. The bartender spoke. "Sure took this one a long time to go down. The stuff usually works quicker."

It took Gabe a moment to make sense of the words. Drugged! He'd been drugged!

There were other voices. Hands took hold of him, began to drag him across the floor. He tried to struggle, but nothing worked. It was as if he were paralyzed.

Bright sunlight suddenly shone into his eyes. It hurt. He was rolled onto his back again. Hands began to move over him. He was being robbed.

A hand probed beneath his duster. "Damn," a man muttered. "This one's loaded for bear."

Besides the pistol on his right hip, Gabe wore another pistol beneath his right armpit, in a special holster that also contained a knife sheath. He felt both the pistol and the knife being removed.

Someone had hold of his right hand. "No wonder he's a lefty," a voice said. "Look at this trigger finger. Bent right out to the side. Ain't good for much 'cept maybe scratchin' ears."

Gabe felt a twinge of pain in the broken finger. He wanted to call out, Bastards! Bastards! But the dizziness was getting worse. He fought it for a moment. Then there was only . . . blackness.

CHAPTER TWO

The pain in Gabe's head as he awoke was excruciating. He started to groan, but caution silenced the sound before it had fully formed. He slowly opened his eyes. Bright sunlight razored more pain into his brain, but he forced himself to leave his eyes open.

He was lying on the ground, in an alley behind a building. Probably behind the saloon. It all came back at once, the drugging, the bartender, the men robbing him. Instantly rage flooded through him. He started to jump to his feet, but he was far too weak and dizzy. He fell back into the dust.

Voices. Someone was coming. Instinctively he rolled into a patch of high grass a few feet away. The grass partly concealed a ditch. He settled down into the ditch, brushing the grass erect above him, hugging the ground closely.

Two men; he could tell by the voices. "Ah, hell, where is the son of a bitch?" one voice said querulously. "Ain't this where we left him?"

A moment's silence. "Musta got up an' gone away."

"Hell, that stuff Josh feeds 'em usually keeps 'em out a lot longer. This yahoo was tough, though. Josh said it took him a long time to go out."

"Why the hell are we out here in the hot sun, any-how?" the other man said in a surly voice. "If he's up and gone, all the better."

"That's the way I feel. But Josh wants us to look. Says the guy made him nervous. Kept sayin' somethin' about his eyes."

The other man chuckled. "He was a big, mean-lookin' bugger, all right. Got Josh's wind up, I s'pose. But hell, he's just one man. An' he ain't got his guns no more, has he?"

"I think that's another thing bothered Josh. All those guns. Must be some kinda gunfighter."

There was another moment's silence. "Hell," the other man said, "I don't wanna tangle with no gunfighter."

"But like you said, he ain't got his guns no more," his companion said irritably. "Won't give us no hassle. We're just s'posed to knock him on the head, an' drop him in a hole somewheres."

"I dunno," the other man said nervously. "I don't go for killin' nobody. Liftin' their stuff's one thing, but, well . . . killin' . . . "

"Josh said to do it," the first man snapped. "You don't wanna buck Josh, do you? An' you know we cain't get in no trouble. Not the way things are fixed. Come on . . . let's find that bozo. Maybe he crawled off to that old shack over there."

Gabe heard the men walk away. He continued to lie quietly. The pain in his head had lessened, so he could think more clearly now. He could plan. Obviously, rob-bing strangers was a well-established part of the saloon's business. Gabe wondered how they could get away with it so openly. Josh must be the bartender. Gabe felt rage smolder inside himself again as he thought of the man who'd drugged him. The worst thing about it all was putting the drug in his root beer. He hoped it hadn't per-manently ruined his taste for root beer. That would be worth killing for.

He had other complaints that would justify killing. He wanted his belongings back. Especially the Sharps. It had been given to him by a very close friend. Closer than a friend, more like a father. The question was, how to do it? He was unarmed, in a strange place, and there were at least three of them.

Gabe had been trained for war from childhood. Among the People, war was a constant, a part of daily life, not only for defense and aggression, but as a man's only true vocation, other than hunting. When a straight charge was called for, when it was an open fight, he'd been trained to ride in hard, directly at the enemy. And when it was not an open fight, when the odds were against him, he'd been trained to use every bit of guile and cunning possible to gain his objective: the defeat of his enemy.

He'd have to get back into the saloon before they disposed of his belongings. Then get the hell out of town. He raised his head a little so that he could see through the grass. The saloon, if that was the building he was lying behind, had a back door. That would be the best way in. The big problem was the two men looking for him. He could hear their voices about fifty yards away. A door creaked, then slammed. They had obviously not found him inside the old shack. He held himself completely still, listening. He heard one of the men, the dominant one, say, "He ain't here, Jed. Coulda gone either way. I'll head down toward the livery stable, you cut back up the alley. See if he's hidin' out in the weeds. Hell, maybe the son of a bitch already done gone and died. It's happened before. Josh ain't too careful with that potion of his."

Mutterings, then Gabe heard footsteps approaching. Grass rustled. Apparently, as ordered, the man was probing through the weeds. He was doing it damned reluctantly. Gabe could hear his grumbling more clearly now. He obviously doubted he'd find anyone. Which would make his search lackadaisical. His eyes would lack sharpness, his brain would be working slowly.

Gabe made himself melt into the ground. In his mind he formed an image of himself as part of the ground, as just another clump of grass. He tried to feel as if he were actually part of what was around him, he merged into it, became it, became invisible. When he'd been with the People, he'd often used this tactic to stalk game. He had once lain within a few feet of a mountain lion without the animal knowing he was there.

The man, the one he called Jed, was moving nearer. Now he was right next to Gabe. He moved the grass aside, and for a moment he saw nothing there but grass and dirt. Until he noticed the eyes. The cold, hard eyes, staring up at him.

Jed jerked backward, but it was already too late. Gabe was leaping erect, standing up into Jed. A hard fist sank into Jed's stomach, to stifle any outcry. Jed grunted in agony and doubled up, wheezing for air. Gabe struck him in the throat, then smashed the heel of his hand against Jed's temple. Jed toppled over, his eyes crossed. Gabe followed him down. His hands settled around Jed's neck, ready to crush his throat.

He hesitated. Better not to kill. Not yet. Not until he knew more clearly what he was facing. He hammered a blow to Jed's other temple. Jed's body jerked, then he lay very still, his breath snoring noisily through a slack throat. He would probably be unconscious for some time . . . if those two blows hadn't already killed him.

Gabe glanced quickly down the alley. No sign of the other man; he'd probably gone to the livery stable, like he'd told Jed. There was no one else in sight. Gabe headed straight for the saloon's back door. Might as well go right on in. Probably the last thing anyone would expect.

The door opened easily. Gabe walked straight inside. It was the saloon, all right. The two drunks who'd been there earlier were still slumped over their tables. And Josh, the bartender, was behind the bar.

Moving silently on moccasined feet, Gabe was halfway to the bar before Josh saw him. Josh turned casually, then, when he saw who it was, saw the way Gabe was heading straight toward him, his eyes bulged and his face paled. "Jesus Christ!" he burst out.

Josh made a grab for something under the bar. As Gabe had expected, he came up with a sawed-off shotgun, but by then Gabe had taken hold of the neck of an empty bottle that had been sitting on the bar, and smashed it against Josh's wrist. Gabe heard bone crunch. Josh screamed, and half dropped the shotgun. It went off with a deafening roar, shattering a whole shelf of glasses behind the bar.

Gabe tore the shotgun away from Josh, tossed it aside, then dragged Josh up onto the bar by his throat. Gabe was aware of the two drunks running toward the front door. Let them go, he thought.

Gabe's hands were clamped around Josh's throat. He watched the bartender slowly turn purple. Sprawled half across the bar, with his feet off the ground and his back bent backward, Josh could not defend himself. "My belongings," Gabe said in a cold, flat voice. "I want what you took from me. I want all of it, right now, or you're a dead man."

He saw that Josh had correctly read his death in Gabe's eyes. He was ready to talk. Gabe loosened his hold a little. "They . . . aren't here," Josh managed to croak, grabbing at his bruised throat. "He already has them. Everything."

Gabe was puzzled. There had been an emphasis on Josh's use of the word *He*. As if he were speaking about God. Gabe was about to ask him where he could find "He" when he heard a door crash open behind him, followed by the pounding of feet. "Goddamn it, Josh," a voice bellowed. "How the hell did he get in here?"

"Just get him off me!" Josh screamed. Gabe turned. He'd recognized the voice; it was the man who'd gone toward the livery stable. He was launching himself at Gabe now. He was a big man, and he was swinging a meaty fist at Gabe's head.

Gabe let go of Josh, blocked the blow, and hit the other man hard in the lower ribs. The man let out a loud "Oof!" then staggered a little to the side. Gabe kicked him in the groin, then hit him hard on the side of the head. A blast of pain through his knuckles made him wish he'd chosen a target involving a little less bone.

But the man was going down, slack-kneed. Gabe turned quickly. As he'd expected, Josh had scrambled over the bar and was heading for the shotgun. Gabe was right behind him, and as Josh bent for the gun, Gabe kicked him right below the ass, between his legs, sinking his toes in deep.

Josh screamed and staggered forward, past the shotgun. Gabe pushed it under a table, then ran after Josh, kicking him again, so that Josh fell on his face. Gabe leaped on his back, pinning him, then grabbed his hair and chin and began forcing his head back. "Tell me where I can find my belongings," he said in a deadly voice, "or I'll break your neck."

Gabe, consumed by rage, was vaguely aware of movement near the door. For the moment he didn't care; a killing mood had swept over him. In another second he would go ahead and break this man's neck. Josh would never drug another traveler.

The thunderous roar of a shot brought Gabe back to sanity. He looked up, still holding on to Josh. Two men were walking toward him. The man in front held a smoking pistol in his right hand. Both men wore stars pinned onto their shirts. "Hold it right there, mister," the man in front snapped. "That first shot went into the ceiling. The next'll go right through your head."

The law. Gabe had never thought of this town as having any law. Not a town where strangers were drugged and robbed openly in a public place. Yet, here the law was . . . with a gun in his hand, now aimed straight at Gabe's head.

Gabe reluctantly let go of Josh, and slowly stood up. "This man robbed me, Sheriff," he said. He'd seen the word *Sheriff* on the man's badge. "Drugged and robbed me. I came in here to get my belongings back."

The pistol was no longer pointing at Gabe, which made him feel a lot better. Maybe the sheriff believed him, maybe he already had his suspicions about Josh. Gabe watched the pistol barrel rise. Then keep on rising. The sheriff's gun hand went high, over the sheriff's head. And then the pistol's long barrel was coming straight down at Gabe's skull. He tried to twist out of the way, but the other man, probably a deputy, had gotten around behind him, and was holding his wrists.

The pistol barrel landed. Pain shot through Gabe's head, and for the second time in an hour he was swallowed by unconsciousness.

CHAPTER THREE

The next time Gabe regained consciousness, his head hurt much worse than it had the first time. He managed to stifle a groan, but even before he opened his eyes, his hand went gingerly to his head, and came away sticky with blood.

He was lying on something lumpy, but not as hard as the ground. He let his eyes open into slits. He immediately saw that he was in a jail cell, lying on a cot. "What the . . . ?" he muttered, then remembered the sheriff's gun barrel crashing down onto his head.

There'd been a mistake. The bartender and his men should be the ones in jail. He'd tell the sheriff, he'd tell him again. He started to get to his feet, swayed dizzily, then realized that he was not the only one in the cell. A thin, dirty-looking man with a scraggy growth of four- or five-day-old beard was lying on a bunk on the far side of the cell. The man was grinning at him. Fairly sympathetically. "What they got you in here for, stranger?" the man asked.

"I don't know," Gabe muttered. He walked to the barred door, began to shake it, while calling out, "Hey! There's been a mistake! I want to talk to someone!"

No response. He shook the door harder, so that it crashed back and forth on its hinges.

"I wouldn't do that if I was you, mister," the other man said, no longer grinning. "If you go an' make Sheriff Cleary mad . . . or Buck—Hell, Buck's even worse."

Gabe did not stop his banging and shouting. It finally seemed to be having results. He heard cursing from up front. Footsteps headed in his direction. Two big men turned a corner in the corridor and walked rapidly toward the cell, scowling. "Oh, lordy," Gabe heard his cellmate mutter. "Both of 'em. The sheriff and Buck."

Both approaching men wore stars pinned to their shirts. Gabe recognized the two men who'd come into the bar. It was the older one who'd hit him, the one with the star that said "Sheriff." "What the hell's goin' on here?" the sheriff bellowed.

"That's the right question," Gabe shot back. "Why am I in this cell? It should be—"

"Shut up!" the sheriff roared. "What the hell are you doing in my jail? That's what you're askin'? Hell, you bust up the saloon, nearly kill three men, and you got the balls to ask why you're here? Somethin' wrong with your brain, mister?"

"It wasn't that way," Gabe insisted. "The bartender doped me, robbed me. Him and the others. I just went back to get what was mine. They should be in here, not me."

Sheriff Cleary smiled. It was not a pleasant smile. He turned to his deputy. "You hear that, Buck? Man's out of his mind."

Buck snickered. "Yeah. Maybe we oughta charge him with slander, too, Sheriff, talkin' 'bout ol' Josh that way. Pillar o' the community, Josh."

Buck snickered again. Gabe studied the two men. They were both big. Cleary, a few years older, had run toward fat, but under the fat there were still muscles. His face was blotched, reddish, indicating an addiction to strong drink. Gabe had detected a slight Texas accent. Gabe hesitated. That was bad news. How did one reason with a Texan?

Buck, on the other hand, appeared to be all Southern cracker, a towering, muscular bull, short on brains, brutal, ignorant. It would be stupid to even think of reasoning with a man like Buck. On the other hand, within the sheriff's little piglike eyes, Gabe thought he could detect a glimmering of intelligence. "Sheriff," Gabe said angrily, "give me a chance and I'll prove they robbed me. There were witnesses. . . . "

"Yeah? Who?"

Gabe's voice trailed away as he remembered his witnesses. Two drunks. Maybe they'd even been in on it. He remained gripping the bars, his face bleak.

"Get back to your bunk," Cleary snapped.

Gabe held his ground. "Not until you've heard me out."

The sheriff looked at Buck. "This one's gonna be trouble," the sheriff said, sadly.

Buck grinned. "Nothin' we can't handle, Sheriff," he replied.

To Gabe's surprise, the sheriff turned and walked away, disappearing around the bend in the corridor, while Buck remained just outside the cell door, still grinning at Gabe. The sheriff was back in less than a minute, carrying a sawed-off, double-barreled, ten-gauge shotgun. Which he proceeded to point directly at Gabe's belly. Gabe noticed that the sheriff also had a set of chains slung over his shoulder. "Up against the back wall of the cell," the sheriff said coldly. "If you don't move, and move real fast, I'll splatter you all over the place. I hate messes, but by God, if you stay by that door, I'll kill you where you stand."

That was the longest speech Gabe had heard the sheriff make. And it was an impressive one. He hesitated only a moment. He heard the man behind him say softly, "Move, mister, 'cause he'll sure as hell do it."

Gabe, his face expressionless, turned around and walked toward the cell's back wall. "Good for you, Billy," he heard Buck say to his cellmate. Gabe turned around, his back to the wall. Buck was grinning at Billy, who tried to grin back, but only succeeded in looking scared.

Buck took out a big ring of keys, then unlocked the cell door. He walked over to the sheriff, took the chains from his shoulder, then walked into the cell.

The sheriff remained in the corridor, the twin muzzles of his shotgun poking between the bars, still trained on Gabe. Buck walked by Billy, and as he did so, he put his hand in Billy's face and pushed, still grinning, sending Billy crashing back against the brick wall. Buck didn't even bother to look. "Hold out your hands," Buck said to Gabe.

Gabe thought of refusing. But why? He now had one of them in the cell with him. If Buck got just a little closer it would be hard for the sheriff to shoot without hitting his deputy. Maybe now was the time to make a break for it.

But Buck stepped to one side, out of the line of fire. "I said hold out your hands," Buck repeated, his grin fading. Gabe hesitated only a moment more. There were two of them, they were both big men, he still felt weak and dizzy from the aftereffects of the drugging and the blow to his head . . . and there was that shotgun. He held out his hands. Buck quickly clapped manacles onto his wrists. The manacles were joined by a length of chain. Another length of chain was fastened around Gabe's waist, and the chain linking the manacles was fastened to it. "Down," Buck said, pushing him back toward the bunk. The edge of the bunk hit Gabe behind the knees, and he sat down hard. Buck put manacles on his ankles, also joined by a short length of chain. He'd only be able to take short, hobbled steps.

Buck was standing over Gabe. "How do you like them apples, big mouth?" he asked, grinning again. He took hold of the wrist chains, and hauled Gabe to his feet. The manacles bit painfully into Gabe's wrists; he had to stand up. "We don't like smartasses round these here parts," Buck said, his grin much colder now. He slapped Gabe twice across the face. "You give me any more excuses, I'll use your fuckin' head for a punchin' bag. You unnerstan'?"

When Gabe said nothing, Buck slapped him again. "I ast you, asshole . . . do you unnerstan'?"

Gabe nodded slowly. Yes, he understood. He understood that someday he would kill this man. Buck must have read the thought in Gabe's eyes. Those cold, expressionless eyes. "Why, you . . . " he started to snarl, drawing his right hand back, fist doubled.

"Let it lie, Buck," the sheriff said in a bored voice. "Let's get back to our card game."

Buck took another long venomous look at Gabe, pushed him back down onto the bunk, then left the cell. Gabe didn't even look up when he heard the cell door being locked. He sat and stared at the far wall as the footsteps of the two lawmen faded away down the hall.

Billy was looking at him. "Josh got to you. Robbed you," Billy said matter-of-factly.

"Yeah," Gabe muttered. "Thought I'd get justice, once the law showed up."

Billy laughed. Bitterly. "Guess you don't know the score round these parts. There ain't no justice. Just Sheriff Cleary. Justice is what he says it is. He's in cahoots with Josh, you know. Shares the loot with him. Hell, takes the lion's share, 'cause he protects Josh. If somebody Josh drugs an' robs kicks up a fuss, the sheriff takes care of the problem. I'm real surprised he didn't just shoot you. For resisting arrest. Seen it happen before."

Gabe looked up slowly. He should have known; it all fit. Nobody could have acted as openly as the bartender and his men without some kind of protection. He remembered how Josh had told him that "He" already had his belongings. "He" was undoubtedly Sheriff Cleary.

What a fool he'd been! Charging into the saloon with no preparation, no planning. He knew better than that. Maybe it had been the drug, maybe it had confused him. He remembered the dizziness, the sense of disorientation after he'd come to. He'd reacted, just reacted to his anger. He'd been foolish, and now he was paying for it.

Gabe only spent a day in the cell. They let Billy go later that day; he was in for drunk and disorderly. Billy had wryly labeled himself the town drunk. He was likable, but weak, Gabe decided. But in a whole lot less trouble than himself.

The morning of the second day, Buck came to the cell and dragged Gabe out by his chains. "Judgment day for you, ol' hoss," Buck said cheerfully.

Nobody seemed to pay much attention as Buck marched Gabe along the dusty main street; most people turned their eyes away. But as they passed the saloon, Gabe looked up and saw Josh standing in the doorway, glaring in his direction. Even at this distance Gabe could see the livid bruises around the other man's throat. He wished he'd killed him. Of course, if he had, he'd be in a whole lot more trouble. The one smart thing he'd done was not kill anybody. If he had, he was positive they'd be hanging him pretty soon. They might anyhow.

They stepped up onto the boardwalk in front of a small building. A faded sign over the door read T. SMITH. JUSTICE OF THE PEACE. Buck prodded Gabe in through the doorway.

There was not much room inside; a couple of chairs stood in front of a desk, behind which sat a man in his fifties or sixties, it was hard to tell. A man with gray hair and a drink-ravaged face. He did not look at Gabe.

Gabe expected to be shoved into one of the chairs, or at least for Buck to sit down. But Buck and the man behind the desk seemed to be waiting for something. A moment later Gabe heard boot heels pounding on the boardwalk outside. Sheriff Cleary came striding into the room, holding a piece of paper. "Hi, Tom," the sheriff said to the man behind the desk, apparently the justice of the peace.

"Hi, John," the man replied, looking up. He finally deigned to notice Gabe. "What kinda problem we got here, John?"

"Troublemaker. Busting up the saloon. Attempted murder on the bartender and two saloon employees. Resisting arrest."

"My, my," the justice of the peace said mildly. "A real bad one. Well . . . we know how to handle bad ones, don't we, John?"

The sheriff nodded. The justice of the peace looked at Gabe again. "What's your name, mister? I don't see it on this here paper."

"Guess I forgot to ask him, Tom," the sheriff said, smiling.

Gabe thought of not answering. But why bother? "Conrad," he said tersely. "Gabe Conrad."

The justice of the peace nodded sagely, pursing his lips. "Well, Mr. Conrad. You're charged with some pretty serious offenses. And that calls for some serious punishment."

"Don't I get to talk to a lawyer?" Gabe asked.

The justice of the peace looked annoyed at being interrupted. The proceedings were probably keeping him from his morning drinking. No . . . they weren't. Gabe watched as the justice of the peace opened a drawer in his desk, took out a pint bottle, and sipped from it. "You got any money for a lawyer, Mr. Conrad?" he asked.

The sheriff broke in. "Not a penny, Tom. He's just another drifter. Tried to rob Josh and his boys."

"That does it, then," the justice of the peace said. "I find you guilty, Gabe Conrad, and I hereby sentence you to . . ." He looked down at the papers again. The sheriff stepped forward and pointed out a couple of lines of writing. "To six months' imprisonment at hard labor," the justice of the peace continued. "To be served on the county penal work force. Starting now. Take him away, Buck."

The justice of the peace seemed to be satisfied, but not the sheriff. He stepped forward again and pointed to several more lines of writing. Tom screwed up his eyes, reading with his lips moving. "Oh, yeah," he said. "All of the prisoner's belongings to be confiscated as a fine. Personal effects to go to the man he attacked, Josh Peters. Horse and horse gear to go to the county, for costs. Case dismissed. Get him out of here."

Buck hustled Gabe toward the door. So fast. It had all happened so fast. My God, they'd even divided up his stolen belongings right in a court of law. What a system they had.

Out in the street Gabe realized he had hit bottom. He'd been robbed of everything he owned, and he was about to spend six months on a chain gang. That's what the sentence meant.

As Buck marched him back toward the jail, Gabe saw that Josh, the bartender, was still standing in the saloon's doorway. Gabe saw Buck wink at Josh. Josh smiled evilly at Gabe. Gabe gazed back steadily. Someday, bartender . . . poisoner, Gabe thought. Someday, just you and me.

Josh, unable to meet Gabe's flat stare, moved back into the doorway. Buck prodded Gabe roughly. "Move along," he snarled.

Gabe turned to stare at Buck. Someday, you, too, he thought. Someday, all of you bastards.

CHAPTER FOUR

The chain gang was not Gabe's first encounter with imprisonment. When he'd been only a boy he'd spent three years in an army guardhouse for trying to kill an army captain. Or so the captain had said. Gabe knew better. The captain had tried to shoot him. Gabe had fought back. The captain had lost the fight, ending up with a pitchfork tine pinning his gun hand to the ground.

But who would believe a half-wild stable boy, who bore the additional stigma of having grown up among Indians? So Gabe had gone to the guardhouse. Unjustly. And now he was going unjustly to a chain gang. But damned if he'd do the six months. He'd die first. No one was ever going to lock him up again. Not for long.

But he let none of his feelings show as he was transported to the camp where the county's prisoner work force lived. It was time to start using his head, so he went meekly. Not much chance of escaping at the moment, anyhow. Buck and another deputy rode alongside the wagon in which Gabe and another prisoner were seated. Both deputies carried sawed-off shotguns across their saddles. Besides, both prisoners wore a mass of chains, which were anchored to ring bolts inside the wagon.

The work camp was five miles out of town. It wasn't much to look at, a collection of largish board shacks, surrounded by a high barbed-wire fence. Gabe noticed two guards patrolling the fence, while another was positioned in a low tower that overlooked the entire camp. There was only one gate.

The prisoners were unbolted from the wagon. Buck rode close as Gabe stood up. "Well, big mouth," Buck sneered, "looks like the county's gonna get a little benefit outta you at last."

Gabe, in his new role of cowed prisoner, said nothing, just kept his eyes downcast. It did him little good. Buck grabbed his wrist chains and dragged him out of the wagon. Gabe fell onto the dirt, while Buck laughed. Once again, Gabe refused to look up. Buck turned to one of the camp guards. "Brought you a real pussy."

Again Gabe said nothing, but allowed himself to be led inside with the other prisoner. The camp seemed oddly deserted. Gabe guessed that the prisoners must be out working. He and the other man were led into one of the buildings by two guards, where they were chained to bunks. The guards went back outside without leaving them anything to eat or drink, and it was a hot day.

"Bastards," the other prisoner murmured scornfully as the guards filed outside. "I see nothing's changed around here."

Gabe looked at the man with interest. He was thin, of medium height, with mousy hair. But his eyes were not mousy; they burned with a hot light. "You've been here before?" Gabe asked.

The man's eyes jerked toward Gabe. They were filled with resentment, and for a moment Gabe thought he would not answer. But he did. "Yeah. Last year. For six months. For coldcocking one of Cleary's fucking deputies. Goddamn if they didn't make me pay for that."

The man, moving with difficulty because of his manacles, managed to tug the back of his shirt upward. Gabe saw a profusion of welted, crisscrossed scars. "Whipped me, the bastards. I won't let 'em do that again. Not ever."

"Why'd you get sent here this time?" Gabe asked.

The man smiled. It changed his whole face, and now Gabe could see the intelligence in the man's eyes, not just the bitterness. "I got a little drunk one night. Said some interesting things about our beloved sheriff. His deputies came for me, and I coldcocked another one. Got a year this time."

And now his smile faded. "They'll never let me finish the year out. Not alive. Not after the things I said."

He straightened his shoulders. "Won't let 'em break me, though, goddamn it. I was born free and I'll die free." He shook his wrists. "These fucking chains don't mean a thing."

As the day wore on, they had little to do but talk. Gabe learned that his fellow prisoner's name was Charles. Not Charlie, but Charles. He insisted on that. Charles Beaufort. Gabe had the impression of a survivor from a good family that had fallen on hard times. Probably ruined by the war. Charles was not the kind of man who'd accept any guff from other men. A handicap in this part of the territory. "Cleary runs the whole damned county," Charles said bitterly. "Plunders it. I heard about you getting taken at the saloon. That's just one of his little setups. I don't know why he even bothers with it anymore. Penny-ante stuff. He gets a lot more out of stolen stock, payoffs, and outright graft. Like this chain gang. It works on projects, supposedly county projects, but the lion's share of the profits go to Cleary. I guess some men are just born greedy; they'll stick with anything that brings in even a little money. Like drugging and robbing strangers in a saloon."

"And the county puts up with this?" Gabe asked. "People don't complain?"

Charles grinned. "Not the ones who want to stay off this chain gang. Or stay alive. Once a man like Cleary's on top, he can figure ways to stay there. Sheriffs have a lot of power in out-of-the-way places like this."

Gabe nodded. He'd never had much use for the law. Not white man's law. It was usually there to keep the power in the hands of those firmly on top. Which was why he did his best to be his own law. Why were white men so greedy? He'd never understood their insatiable desire to have more. Of course, it had once been pointed out to Gabe that he'd been brought up as a nomad. To have more meant you had to carry more every time the tribe moved. Still, why so *much* greed?

Just before sundown Gabe heard sounds from outside, the rhythmic clinking of chains and the shuffle of feet, accompanied by the harsh voices of two or three men. There was a window a few feet away. He got up and, using his chain, dragged the bunk he was fastened to as close to the window as he could get.

A line of about a dozen shackled men were coming in through the gate. They were very dirty, and looked exhausted. A cart trailed them. The cart was loaded with picks, shovels, and other tools. Three guards walked alongside the prisoners, each armed with a shotgun. Gabe noticed that one of the guards was particularly large, a huge man with massive, sloping shoulders and a bald, bullet head. From the way he was shouting orders, he seemed to be the man in charge.

From his bunk, Charles said, "Sounds like Bull. Can you see him? Huge bastard?"

"Yeah."

"He's the one put these scars on my back."

Gabe turned. Charles's face was bleak. "Someday," he murmured. "Someday the bastard's gonna turn his back. And I'll have a pick or an ax in my hands. . . . "

Charles let his voice trail away. A moment later the work gang began to file into the hut, shepherded by Bull and another guard. Bull stopped short when he saw Charles. A huge grin spread over his heavy, bovine features. "Well, well, well," he said. "Knew you wouldn't be able to stay away."

He walked straight toward Charles, who, still sitting on his bunk, stared directly up into the big man's eyes. It was a challenging, hate-filled stare. Gabe saw Bull's face flush. "Goddamn you!" Bull shouted. "Stand up when I'm talking to you!"

He jerked Charles to his feet by his wrist chains. Charles did not cry out, but Gabe could see where the manacles had sliced into the skin. Bull glared down at the smaller man. "We'll get this straight from the start,"

Bull snarled. "You give me any crap this time, I won't waste time whipping you. I'll kill you on the spot."

Charles said nothing, just continued to look straight into Bull's piglike little eyes. Bull suddenly backhanded Charles, knocking him down onto his bunk. And still Charles continued to meet the other man's steady gaze.

Bull whirled on Gabe. "What other kinda garbage did they send me?" he snarled.

Gabe was careful not to meet Bull's eyes. It was not out of cowardice, but because, among the People, he'd been brought up to believe it was impolite to look straight at another man, to pin him with your gaze. To do so was to issue a challenge, or to show contempt, and he was not yet ready to do that. Not yet.

But, like most white men, Bull read Gabe's failure to meet his eyes as lack of guts. "Big," he said, scornfully appraising Gabe, "but a pansy."

With a snort of contempt, Bull left the room. Charles was the only one who saw the answering contempt in Gabe's eyes as Bull walked away. Gabe loathed bullies. He looked up to see Charles smiling at him. "Old Bull's gonna get a surprise one of these days, ain't he?" he said, so softly that only Gabe could hear. Gabe did not reply, just kept staring at the door through which Bull had disappeared.

Like most repressive regimes, the work camp guards enforced a rigid routine. The men were awakened at dawn, brought bread and water by an unshackled trusty, then unchained from their bunks and led outside, where they were divided up for the day's work. Seldom did all of the prisoners work on the same project.

The work was backbreaking, from sunup to just before dark, seven days a week. The food was barely enough to maintain sufficient strength to work. Prisoners who had been in the camp for more than a couple of months were walking skeletons. "Cleary hates to dig into his profits to feed us," Charles said bitterly to Gabe.

Gabe spent the first few days getting used to the routine, never opening his mouth when a guard was near, but taking in and cataloging in his mind every detail of the routine, where each guard stood, when they took breaks, what their personalities were like.

Their personalities were mostly bad. They were all brutal men, the most brutal being Bull, who casually struck or whipped prisoners, apparently just for the pleasure of it. Gabe noticed that Bull kept most of his blows for Charles, who accepted them without a whimper, staring back at Bull all the time.

Gabe was not struck until his third day. He'd been bending low, trying to wrestle a large rock out of the ground, to clear the right-of-way for the wagon road they were building, when, without warning, Bull struck him with the cat-o'-nine-tails he habitually carried. "Goddamn it," Bull snarled. "Put some back into it."

The pain was excruciating, but Gabe did not cry out. He had been trained almost from birth never to cry out from pain, only from exultation or grief, and only when it was the correct time to do so.

He straightened slowly, and now, for the first time, he looked Bull straight in the eye, a look of such piercing hostility that the big guard, who had not been expecting such a look from this meek and obedient prisoner, took a half step backward.

Bull half raised his whip, but he did not strike again. "Get your ass back to work," he growled, and strode on down the line, where he struck the first man that got in his way.

Gabe watched him go. He now knew for sure that whether he escaped or not, Bull would have to die. Even if it cost Gabe his own life. There was no greater shame to a man of the People, to a warrior, than being whipped like a dog.

But how to go about it? There were always at least two guards in sight, one backing up the other, their shotgun muzzles tracking restlessly over the chain gang.

Gabe's chance came when he'd been on the gang for a week. There were ten other men working in his group, including Charles. There were only two guards, Bull and another man. Cleary had so many projects going that the guard force was stretched thin. Apparently Cleary even pinched pennies on security.

The other guard was a cadaverous-looking specimen who obviously had taken the job so that he could torment his fellow humans. A sadistic man. And a drunk. It was against regulations, but the man nipped all day from a bottle he usually kept hidden on his person. But, working with Bull, he didn't dare keep the bottle on him. Gabe had seen the guard secret the bottle behind some bushes, about forty yards from where the chain gang was working. From time to time, under guise of answering the call of nature, the guard would walk off toward the bushes. And his bottle.

Gabe had noticed. So had Charles. They exchanged glances. All of the men had been unchained from one another, so that they could work more freely. Gabe and Charles slowly worked closer to each other until they were able to start working together as a team. Charles was using a pick to loosen rocks, while Gabe dragged them from the right-of-way and stacked them in piles.

Twice during the afternoon the alcoholic guard made a trip to his bottle. But each time, Bull was at the far end of the line of working men. It was not until the day was nearly over that the man's trip to the bushes coincided with Bull's presence close to Gabe and Charles.

They had him more or less sandwiched between them, but not quite closely enough. Bull was watching Charles sink his pick into the ground, while behind him, Gabe was stacking rocks. Gabe began to edge forward. If he could only get a little closer . . .

Then Bull noticed that the other guard was nowhere in sight. "Where the fuck did Sims go?" he muttered aloud, looking up and down the line of toiling men.

Damn. In another couple of seconds he'd walk away, looking for Sims. He had to be stopped. Bull's back was to Gabe, but if Gabe tried to rush him, Bull would hear the clanking of his leg irons. "To dig up his bottle, you fat, stupid son of a bitch," Gabe said in a cutting, sarcastic voice.

The words worked wonders. Bull spun around to face Gabe. "What? What the hell did you say?" he roared, his mouth hanging open in surprise. "Why, you . . ."

Bull started toward Gabe, his whip held high, his shotgun trailing in his other hand. Behind him, Charles, a snarl of hatred on his face, launched himself at Bull's broad back, his pick held high over his head, ready to bury the pointed end in Bull's bald skull.

But Bull heard the rattle of Charles's leg chains. Or perhaps it was Charles's muttered curse. Or maybe just the fact that Bull couldn't see his fellow guard, and strange things were happening around him.

Bull spun just in time. For a big man, he was fast. Even as the pick was swinging down toward his head, Bull was trying to bring his shotgun around. He got one of the big twin hammers cocked, but there was not enough time to bring the muzzle to bear on Charles. Bull did the only thing he could: He dropped the shotgun, and reached up to seize the shaft of the descending pick.

When the shotgun hit the ground it went off with a roar, skittering away several feet. Damn, Gabe thought, the noise would bring the other guard. He thought of going for the shotgun, but there was no time. Bull, so much stronger than Charles, had already wrestled the pick away from the smaller man. He knocked Charles down, then, with a bellow of rage and triumph, raised the pick over his head, ready to drive it into Charles's skull.

Gabe leaped forward. Clasping his hands together, he let his wrist chains trail free, then swung both arms hard, lashing the chains against the side of Bull's massive head. Blood spurted. Bull howled, and started to turn. But by now Gabe was on top of him. He doubted the chains were heavy enough to do any permanent damage to Bull's massive skull, so instead of swinging them again, he flung their looped length over the big man's head, then pulled back hard, settling the chains into place around Bull's thick neck.

Fortunately, Bull was a little stunned by the initial blow. Gabe doubted he'd have been able to hold him long enough to set the chain otherwise, but the links now bit into Bull's throat, and Gabe hauled back hard, forcing the other man to backpedal. Bull tried pushing back into Gabe, tried to cause him to lose his balance, but Gabe countered the move by turning his back on

Bull, crossing his wrists, and hauling the bigger man half up onto his back.

Bull began to gag and wretch, and to claw at the chain biting into his throat instead of fighting Gabe directly, a mistake on Bull's part, but Gabe doubted it would make much difference. It took time to strangle a man, and in the meantime the other guard must have heard that damned shotgun go off.

He had. He came running now, levering back both barrels of his ten gauge. He saw Gabe and Bull struggling together and raised the shotgun, but he could not fire immediately for fear of hitting Bull, so he ran farther forward, not noticing until almost too late that Charles, on his hands and knees, was scrambling toward the shotgun Bull had dropped. By the time the guard saw this new peril, Charles had risen to his knees, and was cocking the hammer of the shotgun's unfired barrel. The muzzle of the guard's shotgun swerved from Gabe to Charles. Both guns went off together, both gunners aimed true. The guard spun completely around, Charles's gun having blown away one side of his chest, while Charles was knocked over onto his back by a load of buckshot.

Gabe saw it happen, but there was nothing he could do; he was still locked in a death struggle with Bull, who had taken hold of the chain now, and was trying to tug it away from his throat. But the big man was way off balance. Gabe suddenly heaved on the chains, sending Bull flying half over one shoulder. Keeping a tight hold on the chains, Gabe followed him down, then leaped onto Bull's back as he hit the ground, facedown.

It was simply a matter of time after that. Gabe set his right knee into the center of Bull's back, holding him down while he hauled back on the chains. Bull flailed and fought, but to no avail. The chains dug more and more deeply into his throat, until he was no longer able to breathe. What Gabe could see of the other man's face was beginning to turn purple. His frantic movements became more and more jerky until, at the end, there was only the rapid drumming of his legs against the ground. Then silence.

Gabe kept up the pressure until he was positive the

other man was dead. Only then did he free the chains and
slowly stand up. It took him a little while to get his breath
back, then he bent down and searched through Bull's
pockets for the keys to the chains. It was an unpleasant
task; during the final moments of the struggle, Bull had
lost control of his bladder and bowels; he had fouled
himself.

Gabe quickly unlocked his chains. All of them. Just
in case any other guards might have been near enough
to hear the firing, he ran straight for the other guard's
shotgun; it still had one barrel unfired. Only then, with a
weapon in his hands, did Gabe go over to where Charles
was lying.

A large pool of blood soaked the ground around
Charles's supine body, leaking from his ruined chest.
He was dead, but Gabe noticed that there was a smile
of triumph on Charles's face. Gabe nodded his head in
respect. Here was a man, a warrior.

Gabe turned away. There was nothing he could do for
his friend, it was time to save the living. Time to pay
back those who had chosen to become his enemies. Gabe
tossed the keys to the other prisoners. Some gleefully
clamored for a chance to unlock themselves. Others were
hesitant, unwilling to become fugitives. But the sight of
the two dead guards convinced most; there would be an
orgy of vengeance exacted. It would not be a good idea
to be anywhere near when the bodies of the two dead
guards were discovered.

Carrying the shotgun, Gabe went to the wagon that
carried the tools and unhitched the old nag that drew it. A
sorry beast, but better than being afoot. He sat the horse a
moment, watching the men scamper down the road, each
looking for his own escape route. They'd confuse the
issue, there were no guards alive to tell what had actually
happened. This would look like a mass jailbreak, at least
until the first prisoners were recaptured and forced to tell
what had happened. Everyone would believe that every
prisoner was on his way to a safe hideout.

But one would not be. Gabe turned the old nag toward
town. There were scores to be settled.

CHAPTER FIVE

It was not far to town, which was both good and bad: good, because he'd reach town quickly; bad, because the news of the escape might reach town quickly, too. Eventually, when Bull's gang did not return to the camp, the other guards would come looking for them.

Gabe took a roundabout route to town, avoiding the main road. It was beginning to grow dark by the time he saw the town's ragtag clump of buildings in the distance. He'd been planning along the way. No more bulling straight in. Go in quietly, leave quietly. And he'd have to have a way out. That meant a horse. A better horse than this sorry bucket of bones he was riding.

He'd asked Charles where the sheriff might keep confiscated stock. Charles had given him the location of the county corral. It was out on the edge of town. Gabe turned the nag loose about a hundred yards short of the corral, then worked his way closer on foot. There was always the chance that the sheriff had already sold his horse. But there should be others.

Gabe ghosted in close to the corral. It was almost completely dark now. There was a barn attached to the corral. He waited a while to see if a guard had been posted. He saw no one. If there was a guard, he'd probably gone home for supper.

Gabe slipped into the barn. It took his eyes a little while to get used to the dark. He saw a tack room. There was still a little light, and he was delighted to see his saddle and bridle, plus his rifle scabbards, piled in a corner. No saddlebags, though. That worried him. Gabe was a nomad by both training and inclination and was not attached to objects—except for his mother's family Bible, and his big buffalo hide coat. A part of his soul was contained in each one of them. It filled him with a cold anger to think of another man wearing his Thunderbird coat, or browsing through that Bible. Browsing through his life.

There was the Sharps, too. It had been given to him by a man who had been like a father: Jim Bridger, the old mountain man and scout. He could always buy another Sharps, but not one with the same associations.

The bartender, Josh, must have them. The justice of the peace had awarded him Gabe's personal possessions. Pray God he still had them, because Gabe was going to go looking.

First, transportation. Gabe quietly moved his horse gear out of the stable and secreted it in the brush. Now, a horse. He moved silently toward the corral, carrying his bridle. Wonderful! His horse was still there! It was only justice that he get it back. Besides, it was a fine animal, a little mean, true, but with courage, strength, and great endurance.

Recovering his horse was easy. Anyone raised by the Lakota should be able to steal a horse right out from under the man riding him. Gabe grinned at the image as he stole into the corral. It took a couple of moments to gentle his big stallion, but eventually the animal took the bit without too much complaining.

Gabe led the horse into the brush, where he quickly saddled it, lashing in place his rifle scabbards. He mounted, then rode in a circle around the town, heading for the rear of the saloon.

The horse had been easy. Getting back the rest of his belongings, if they were still in the area, would be a little more difficult. And then there were accounts to be settled, personal accounts. Payment for the way he'd been treated.

One good thing about this miserable little town was that there were not many lights. Gabe was able to tie his horse to a small tree only a few yards from the rear of the saloon, but even so, it was damned difficult to see the animal in the darkness.

Now . . . the saloon itself. If he'd been armed, he might have walked right in the front door. But he only had a shotgun with one barrel loaded. He decided to leave the shotgun with his horse; it might impede a quiet entrance into the saloon.

He'd already ruled out the back door. He remembered that it squeaked, and led straight into the room. He'd be noticed the moment he stepped inside.

But there was a window off to one side of the back door. Gabe moved next to the window and looked inside. As much as the dirty glass would let him see, the window led into a small storeroom.

It took Gabe several moments to pry the window open; it was stuck shut with dirt and old paint. Finally he had it open enough to allow him to slip inside.

The room was very dark, with just a little light filtering in through the window. There was a single door. He tried to visualize the saloon, to remember where that door was. He thought he'd seen a door way off to the side, behind an old piano.

He tried the doorknob. It was old and rusty, a candidate for a squeaky opening. It took Gabe nearly five minutes to turn the knob enough so that the door was no longer latched. He opened it a couple of inches. A thin stream of light leaked into the storeroom. Along with sound. He could hear voices. And he was sure one of the voices belonged to Josh.

Gabe opened the door a little more, until he had it open just far enough to slip through, which he did, staying low, nearly crawling.

He'd been right. There was an old piano just a few feet away. He slipped into its shadow. Hunkered low behind the piano's bulk, he could hear very clearly. Josh was carrying on a desultory conversation with someone

whose voice Gabe didn't know. Gabe's ears pricked up
when the other man said good-bye. Footsteps moved
toward the door, then faded away outside. He couldn't
hear anyone else. This was the time to make his move.

Suddenly there was a commotion outside on the boardwalk. A moment later Gabe heard footsteps pounding
into the saloon. "Josh!" a voice called out. "There's been
a jailbreak. The chain gang. They all got away, including
that big ape who tried to strangle you."

"Jesus, no!" Gabe heard Josh say half under his breath.

"Whatsa matter, Josh?" the other man said, a little
smugly. "You scared of him? Hell, he's probably miles
away by now, lightin' out for other parts with the rest
of them jailbirds. Hey . . . gimme a drink."

Gabe thought he recognized the other voice as belonging to one of the men who'd helped Josh rob him. He
slowly peeked over the top of the piano. Yes, it was the
one he'd hit in the saloon the day he'd been arrested.

"Naw, he doesn't scare me," Josh was saying, with
what Gabe considered false bravado. "Hell, he ain't
even armed. Old Tom awarded me his guns and his
other personal stuff when they sentenced him. Hardly
worth the trouble . . . except for the guns. Just some
worthless junk in the saddlebags, stuff to be thrown
away." He snorted derisively. "Cleary got the best part,
as usual. The horse and saddle."

Gabe stiffened as Josh poured the other man a drink.
He wondered if Josh had already disposed of the "junk,"
his Bible, the Thunderbird coat. He was heartened when
Josh said, "Here . . . I'll show you. Just an old coat, and
somebody's family Bible. The Bible's got a lot of real
small writing in the margins."

He watched Josh reach under the bar and produce his
saddlebags. He pulled out the Bible, which the other man
was uninterested in examining. "The guns were worth
the trouble, though," Josh said, thumping Gabe's holsters down onto the bar top. "That man had more iron
on him than a locomotive."

"Yeah," the other man said, grinning. "That's what
made you nervous. Thinking he might be some big gunfighter. On his way back to pay you a little social visit."

"Let him try. He ain't got his guns, now, has he? I got 'em, and if he comes in here, it'll be his last move. I'll cut him down like a dog with his own lead."

"Yeah. Well, like I said, I figure he's out in the hills with those other jailbirds, runnin' for his life. Sheriff's gettin' up a posse. We're gonna ride out in about half an hour. Wanna come along?"

Josh nodded. "Maybe so. But I gotta close up first. You go and tell the sheriff I'll be ready in a few minutes. Maybe you could drop by the livery stable on the way and ask 'em to saddle up my horse."

"Sure thing." The other man downed his shot of whiskey, then headed for the door. Josh stayed behind the bar, watching him go. When Josh was alone, Gabe heard him mutter, "Sorry state of affairs. That drifter did make me nervous. I'll be glad when I see him dead. God . . . those eyes."

The saloon was empty now, except for Josh. And Gabe, who watched Josh reach under the bar and come up with his shotgun, which he placed on top of the bar. Gabe knew that it was time to make his move, before anyone else came in. He ghosted from behind the piano, bent low, and slipped in behind the bar. He did not straighten up until he was only a few feet from Josh.

To Josh, it seemed as if Gabe materialized out of nowhere. "Shit!" he blurted, his eyes widening in fear. He immediately reached for the shotgun, but by now Gabe had reached his own weapons, which Josh had so thoughtfully stacked on top of the bar. He reached out, not for one of his pistols—he wanted this quiet—but for the razor-sharp knife that rested in a sheath sewn to the side of his shoulder holster. Gabe's left hand held the shotgun pinned to the bar, while his right drove the long thin blade deep into Josh's stomach. Their faces were only a couple of feet apart. Gabe watched Josh's eyes widen in shock as the knife went in. Josh's hands came away from the shotgun and clutched desperately at Gabe.

Gabe ripped the knife sideways, opening a huge hole in Josh's stomach. This man would drug no more thirsty travelers. Josh screamed, a choked, hoarse

cry that Gabe hoped would not travel far. He stepped
back, letting Josh fall. Damn, his hand was sticky with
the other man's blood. He took a moment to wipe
both hand and knife clean with a bar rag. Then he picked
up his saddlebags and quickly crammed the Bible back
inside. Good, his pipe was still in there, too, the one the
old Lakota medicine man, Two Face, had given him the
day the soldiers hanged him.

There was his bedroll, too. Gabe took a moment to
buckle on both his holsters. He checked the pistols
inside the holsters. Fully loaded. Then he picked up the
bedroll, saddlebags, and coat, and headed for the back
door and his horse.

It took only a couple of minutes to fasten his belongings in place, behind his saddle. His horse shifted nervously, perhaps smelling the blood still on Gabe's hands.
The rifles. He had to go back for the rifles. He stepped
in through the back door—and nearly had his head blown
off.

Josh was not yet dead. He'd managed to stagger to his
feet, with half his guts hanging out, and had retrieved the
shotgun. The moment Gabe came in through the door,
Josh let go with both barrels, but Gabe had sensed movement by the bar, and had quickly stepped to one side. The
double load of buckshot shattered half the door behind
him, but before the echoes had died away, Gabe pulled
one pistol from his hip holster, and shot Josh through
the chest.

Josh, already reeling from the shotgun's recoil, fell
full length behind the bar. Gabe ran closer and leaned
over the bar for a closer look. Amazingly, Josh was still
alive, his eyes staring up at Gabe. Gabe aimed his pistol at Josh's head. "No . . . " Josh whimpered, but his
voice was cut off by the roar of the pistol. Josh flopped
backward, half his head blown away, his legs jerking
convulsively against the dirty barroom floor.

Gabe leaned over the bar and grabbed both rifles. Were
they loaded? No time to check; he could hear yelling out
in the street, coming closer to the saloon. The shots had
probably alerted the whole damned town.

Gabe had just started toward the back door when the

saloon's swinging doors crashed open, and the man who'd been talking to Josh earlier, the one who'd helped rob Gabe, ran inside the saloon. He could not see Josh, but there was a regular river of blood running from behind the bar. His eyes flicked to Gabe. "Jesus God!" he burst out, then reached for the pistol on his hip.

Gabe let the rifles fall; he could not take a chance on their being loaded. His own pistol was in his hand again, and before the other man could fire, Gabe leveled the .44, held the trigger back, and fanned the hammer with the heel of his left hand three times, so quickly that it was difficult to distinguish the sound of each separate explosion. The heavy slugs slammed into his opponent's abdomen. The man flew backward, his pistol firing harmlessly into the ceiling. After he hit the floor, he remained motionless.

Two down. Two of the men who'd wronged him were now either dead or dying. But it was time to leave. More footsteps outside. Gabe picked up the Winchester, levered the action. A bright brass cartridge case came flying out. Damned if it wasn't loaded.

None too soon. The swinging doors crashed open again, and a big man rushed inside. Buck. Gabe could see others behind him. It was dim in the saloon, and at first Buck could see no one but the dead man lying on the floor. Then he looked up, staring toward the rear of the saloon. Staring straight into the muzzle of Gabe's Winchester.

Buck had a pistol in his hand but, as Gabe had expected, he was more bully than fighter. "No!" he screamed, crossing his arms protectively over his face, with his pistol aimed harmlessly at the ceiling.

Another man might not have fired. But Gabe had been brought up from infancy to despise a coward. Any man who begged for mercy was a man begging to be killed. How could a coward stand to live? Gabe fired, blowing a hole in Buck's throat. Buck staggered backward, choking on his own blood. Gabe put the next round through his heart, right next to the shiny brass star pinned to his shirt.

Buck was still falling when Gabe changed his aim

toward the swinging doors. Men were swarming up onto the boardwalk, getting ready to rush inside. Gabe thought he could make out the tall, broad form of the sheriff. He fired rapidly, eight shots, right through the doorway. Men shouted, others cursed, but they all dived for cover.

Bending low, Gabe picked up the Sharps, then ran silently toward the back door. Once outside, he shoved the Sharps into its scabbard, then leaped into the saddle, holding onto the Winchester. He leaned backward, rummaged in his saddlebags, and pulled out a handful of .44-40 rounds, which he began stuffing into the Winchester's loading gate. At the same time he was using his knees to urge his horse into motion. Men were already running toward both ends of the alley. He'd have to make his move before they boxed him in.

There seemed to be fewer men to his left. He veered his horse in that direction. As he neared the men, he saw that there were only three or four. Gabe let out a loud whoop, his sound of battle. Standing in the stirrups, he fired several shots from the Winchester. He didn't aim to hit; these might be honest citizens ahead, if any existed in this miserable town. Fortunately, they began to scatter as Gabe pounded down on them.

And now he saw that he had made a mistake. They were not all innocent citizens. The massive bulk of Sheriff Cleary loomed up from the left. Gabe frantically changed his aim, and fired. He was heartened to see Cleary grab his side and spin partway around. A moment later Gabe was out of the mouth of the alley, riding hard for the darkness that ringed the town.

A gun fired behind him. He heard the bullet pass close to his head. He twisted in the saddle and looked back. Cleary may have been hit, but he was not down. He was kneeling in the dirt, leveling a pistol. Gabe twisted in the saddle, and fired his Winchester beneath his right arm, not really expecting to hit Cleary, but maybe shake him up a little, spoil his aim.

It didn't work. Gabe saw flame jet from the muzzle of Cleary's pistol. A moment later a massive blow slammed into Gabe's left shoulder.

CHAPTER SIX

The force of the blow nearly knocked Gabe from his horse. He'd been hit!

Steadying himself by grabbing hold of the saddle horn, Gabe urged the horse onward with pressure from his knees. He had to hold onto the Winchester. Damn, he couldn't. With fumbling fingers he stuffed the rifle into its saddle scabbard. With his hands free, he could ride better, stay on the damned horse. His shoulder was hurting badly now, the initial numbness having changed to a crushing ache. Worse, he could feel wetness running down his back.

From behind him he heard yelling. "Get the horses!" someone was shouting. It sounded like Cleary's voice. They were going to be after him in a minute. With his wound, he'd never outdistance them.

He was nearing a house, one of the few that were scattered loosely around the town. He noticed a small corral. There were two horses inside. No lights showed from the house. Maybe the owner was in town. Maybe he just didn't like lights, and would come outside in a few seconds, shooting.

Gabe had to take the chance. He opened the corral gate from the saddle, stifling a groan as the pain in his shoulder flared. The two horses inside were milling around nervously. He rode inside, then forced one of the horses out through the gate. Gabe was careful to close the gate behind him. The horse he had released stood a few yards away, stamping nervously. Gabe began herding it with his own mount, forcing it away from the corral, into the darkness.

He could hear sounds of pursuit from behind him. He urged his horse forward, still herding the other horse. He remembered a place just outside town, where the trail narrowed to pass through a thicket. It was just ahead but, because of the speed of the pursuit coming from behind him, he wondered if he was going to make it.

He reached the thicket with the sheriff and his men only a couple of hundred yards behind. He stopped in the middle of the trail, then slipped his Winchester from its scabbard, and slowly brought it to his shoulder. The pain in his left shoulder nearly made him drop it, but he gritted his teeth and pulled the trigger.

He fired five shots, levering the action quickly. The range was fairly great, but the bullets he sent their way made the posse members fan out. Most pulled up their horses, not wanting to run in straight against the muzzle of his rifle.

And now he fired a shot just above the ears of the horse he'd been herding. Whinnying in fear, the startled animal took off at a run, straight along the trail.

Gabe quickly forced his own horse into the thicket. He could hear the other horse pounding away down the trail, and from behind came the sound of the posse getting itself together again. There was a little starshine. As he'd hoped, the posse members caught a glimpse of the running animal when it came out the other side of the thicket. "There he goes, boys!" someone shouted. A moment later, the posse was once again in full pursuit.

They thundered by Gabe's hiding place, perhaps twenty of them, whooping, hollering, and firing. The noise and pursuit ought to keep the riderless horse ahead of them running for quite some time.

Gabe waited until he was positive every member of the posse was out of sight and hearing, then he rode out the back side of the thicket and headed cross-country.

They'd eventually realize they'd been tricked, and they'd backtrack until they found where he'd ditched them. But it was night, and following his trail would be difficult. He had until morning to cover his tracks.

Gabe rode steadily for three hours, not making much effort to hide his trail. The ground was too damned soft, anyhow. He rode to a place where he remembered more complex soil, with hard spots, and running water. Only then did he begin covering the signs of his passage, guiding his horse over a jigsaw route that should confuse the posse members even in daylight, unless they had an awfully good tracker.

It was not until he was certain that he had covered his trail that he finally headed in the direction he wanted to go . . . toward the mountains. It was a lot easier to hide out in mountains than in flat, open areas. In the mountains, even if they found his trail, if he was up high enough, he could see them coming from a long way off.

He had to do something about his wound. He had hoped that it would stop bleeding on its own. It had not. He could feel blood seeping slowly down his back.

He dismounted and rummaged in his saddlebags, pulling out an old shirt. He tore the shirt into strips and tried to bind them tightly around his shoulder, without bothering to take off the shirt he was wearing. But it was a hard wound to bind up, the cloth kept slipping, and he was tiring himself with the effort. Finally, only partially satisfied, he remounted his horse and continued toward the mountains, still feeling the slow seepage down his back, although it was not as bad as before.

Dawn found him in the foothills. He headed steadily upslope, until he was surrounded by pine-clad heights. A small valley lay below him. He rode down into it, until it became clear that he was going to have to stop soon; he was growing weaker and weaker. He fumbled for his canteen, tipped it to his mouth. There was only a swallow left, and he needed water. Needed it badly. It was always the same when he lost a lot of blood, this craving for water. He knew there was water nearby, he could smell the wetness. So could his horse. He let the horse's thirst guide him to the water. A spring bubbled

out of the ground below a small rock ledge. Gabe licked
his lips at the sight of the water. He let his horse drop
its head and drink. But if he dismounted, he doubted he
would have the strength to get back up into the saddle.

He had to have that water, though. He slowly dragged
his right leg over the horse's back. It was when he tried to
put his weight onto the left stirrup, and dismount, that he
knew he was not going to be able to control his descent.
His shoulder burned and ached, his head throbbed, and
suddenly the world spun around him. A whirling blackness engulfed Gabe's senses. He knew he was falling but
was unable to do anything about it. Did not even care.

Something was touching his face. Something damp
and cool. Gabe slowly opened his eyes, only to find them
partially covered. He stirred, trying to turn his head away
from whatever was obscuring his vision. It worked. His
vision was a little blurred but, to his amazement, he saw
a face hovering over his own. The face of a young woman. He looked up into large, dark eyes. The girl's hair
was dark, too. He noticed that it was formed into two
large braids. The braids hung down along the side of the
girl's face, framing lovely features.

It was Yellow Buckskin Girl! His Oglala wife. But
she was dead! He'd seen her die, that terrible day on the
Tongue River, when the soldiers attacked Black Bear's
encampment. He'd seen his enemy, Stanley Price, put
a bullet through her head.

Maybe he was dead, too. Maybe that was it. Maybe he'd died from his wound, and gone to the white
man's heaven. But what would Yellow Buckskin Girl,
a Lakota, be doing in the white man's heaven? Or were
there other heavens?

Then the girl said something. In English. And he knew
it was not Yellow Buckskin Girl. His vision cleared a
little. It was the girl's eyes, those large, dark eyes, and
the thick dark braids that had fooled him. The rich tan
of her face, too. But it was still too light a tan, lighter
than Yellow Buckskin Girl's coppery skin.

He felt a crushing sense of loss. "Are you okay?" the
girl was saying. He could not answer, shook his head,

stifled a sound of grief. The girl suddenly stood up, dropping something. He saw that it was a wet handkerchief. She must have been wiping the sweat from his face.

The girl looked down at him for another few seconds. He could not quite decipher her expression. Fear? Fascination? Excitement?

She suddenly spun away. "Mary!" the girl cried out. "Hal!"

He watched her go. She looked even more like Yellow Buckskin Girl from the back, with those heavy braids bouncing against her straight, slender back. He closed his eyes, a mistake, because, unbidden, ugly scenes flowed across his mind. The bullet taking Yellow Buckskin Girl in the forehead. Watching her fall. The carnage in the camp as the soldiers indiscriminately slaughtered men, women, children, the old. He felt a searing blast of hatred for the white man. For all white men. Perhaps for himself, for was he not white, too?

He heard excited voices, the pounding of running feet. He opened his eyes. The scenes of violence and fear were replaced by the sight of three people coming toward him, fast. The girl and a man and a woman.

The man knelt beside him, studied his face. The woman spoke. "His shirt's all bloody in back."

"He's been shot," the man said. He studied Gabe's face again, his own face impassive. He seemed to reach a decision. "Go back to the house. Bring a couple of those pine poles, and some blankets."

The two women started on their way, but Gabe saw the younger one, the one who looked like Yellow Buckskin Girl, stop for a moment and turn back to look at him, that same vivid expression on her face. Then she turned and ran after the other woman.

They were back in a few minutes; the house must not be far. The older woman, she must have been about thirty, was carrying two long poles made of peeled pine. The girl had a stack of blankets.

The man, they called him Hal, set the poles a couple of feet apart, and began interlacing the blankets around them until he had made a serviceable stretcher. "Okay,"

Hal told the women. "You and Becky take his feet, I'll take his shoulders. We'll have to kind of slide him onto this contraption."

Hal, Becky, Mary. Gabe silently repeated their names over and over, to take his mind off the agonizing pain in his shoulder as they half dragged him onto the stretcher. Then they picked him up, the two women at his feet, Hal at his head. "My horse," Gabe murmured, the first words he'd uttered.

"I'll get him later," Hal replied. "I saw him up beyond the spring, grazing. I don't think he'll go far."

He could see the house now, more shack than house, sagging a little to one side. It was situated next to a grove of cottonwoods. A small corral held two horses.

Instead of taking him inside, they put him down on the porch. "There's more light out here," Hal said to the woman called Mary. "We're gonna have to take a look at his wound. Or wounds. He looks like he's bled half to death."

"My God . . . look at all the guns," Mary said. "I wonder who he is."

"Yeah." It was Hal's voice. Gabe was having trouble keeping his eyes open. Then he felt the pistol being removed from his hip holster. His eyes flew open. Hal was looking straight down at him, almost challengingly. Hal's hand went to his shoulder rig; Gabe had not had time to cover it with his duster before leaving the saloon. Gabe's hand started to come up, to stop Hal's. Then he decided to do nothing. His life was in their hands anyhow. Without their help, he knew he would die.

Hal removed not only the pistol and the knife, but also the entire shoulder rig. With the help of the women, he began peeling off Gabe's shirt. "We're gonna have to roll him over," he heard Hal say.

Gabe clamped his teeth tightly as Hal, with the help of the two women, turned him over onto his stomach. He heard cloth ripping as they cut the blood-soaked shirt away from his torso. "Oh, my God!" he heard the girl, Becky, gasp when she saw the wound.

"It's not that bad," Mary reassured her. "Hasn't mortified. See? That purple color is mostly bruising. He's sure lost a lot of blood, though. And I think the bullet's still in there. It's going to have to come out."

There was a reassuring air of competence about the woman's voice. Gabe had an image of her tending to sick animals. A Western woman, brought up to handle any kind of trouble. "Becky, heat up some water," he heard her say. "Hal, take that long, thin knife and run it through the fire. I want it clean."

Time began to drift for Gabe. Was it an hour, or five minutes since the woman had last spoken? Then he was aware of people kneeling around him. He looked up. The girl, Becky, was kneeling very close, right in his line of sight. He saw the concern on her face. She had another handkerchief in her hand. She began wiping his face with it. The handkerchief was wet. It felt good, soothing.

He felt fingers probing near the wound. He started to stiffen, then stopped himself. That would not do. Suddenly, a searing pain. It felt as if someone had stuck a red-hot coal halfway through his back and shoulder. Again, the tendency to stiffen, to cry out, but he fought it back, fought to keep his face impassive.

The pain seemed to go on forever. It felt as if the woman, he was sure it was Mary, wanted to pull him apart. Finally, he heard a heavy clunk, as something solid thudded down onto the wooden porch. "There . . . it's out," he heard Mary say.

They bandaged him, which actually felt good. Protective. Through half-closed eyes, he saw Becky looking at him strangely. "His face didn't show anything at all," she said, the awe plain in her voice. "It had to hurt, didn't it, Mary?"

It was Hal who answered. "There's some damn tough men out here, Becky."

"Wow!" the girl said.

"Tough isn't always the same as good," Hal replied, a warning in his voice. Finally, he added, "I wonder just who the hell he is."

Gabe wanted to tell them, wanted to dispel the concern they must be feeling. But he could not speak. He had to sleep. Right now.

CHAPTER SEVEN

The next three days were a hazy blur to Gabe; he was asleep most of the time, coming to occasionally, not sure what he was seeing. There was often a face hovering over his own, the face he'd seen when he'd regained consciousness near the spring. Once again he confused that face, with its large, dark eyes, and dark braids, with Yellow Buckskin Girl, his Oglala wife. His dead wife. Dead.

Late in the third day he awoke clearheaded. This time it was the woman called Mary who was bending over him. He saw why he had awakened; she was sponging his face and neck. She backed away a little when she saw his eyes open. After studying his face for a moment, she said, "Looks like you're actually with us this time."

Gabe blinked, gathering his wits. "You're called . . . he called you Mary."

"Yes. Mary Jackson. That he you're talking about is my husband, Hal. Now, how are you feeling?"

"Uh . . . better."

"Your shoulder?"

He flexed the wounded shoulder carefully, fought back a wince. It hurt when he moved it. "It'll do," he said noncommittally.

Which Mary picked up. "You don't volunteer much, do you?"

Gabe said nothing for a minute. He remembered their concern when they'd found him, concern over his weapons, over finding a man with a gunshot wound next to their house. He probably owed them his life. Time he acknowledged the debt. "If I were to thank you as much as I should," he said gently, "it would take half the day."

Mary actually blushed a little. "Well . . . we couldn't just let you lie there and bleed to death, could we?"

A little flustered, she looked for something to do. He watched her rinse the cloth she was holding in a basin of water, then wring it out. "Let me pull the blanket down a little," she said. "You've been . . . sweating a lot. You had a fever. I guess there must have been a little bit of infection. Or maybe it was just the loss of blood."

She slid the blanket lower, baring his arms and chest. Gabe realized that he was naked beneath the sheet and blanket. He wondered who had undressed him. He looked across the room and saw the girl, Becky. As if she could read his mind, she blushed.

Mary swabbed at his torso in a very professional manner. He noticed that she was looking at the long, thin scars on his arms and chest. He could see the question growing in her eyes, and anticipated it. "I did it myself," he said. "When my mother and wife were killed. Cut myself with a knife . . . and made a lot of noise. It's an old Oglala custom."

"Oglala?"

"What you call the Sioux, and we call the Lakota. The Oglala are a branch of the Lakota. We lived in what you call South Dakota. And other places you now call by different names."

She smiled. "You talk about 'we,' and 'you.' Are you part Indian, then?"

He shook his head. "No. My body is white. My mother and father were both white, but I was born among the Lakota. After my father's death. My mother and I lived among the Oglala until I was grown."

Mary pursed her lips. "You said your body is white. Did you mean to exclude your mind?"

Gabe let a long silence pass. "I don't know," he finally answered. "A few years ago, I might have said yes. Now . . . the question confuses me. So much has changed . . . "

He could have said, so much has been destroyed. The People . . . herded onto reservations, those who survived. The old ways, the old, free, wild ways gone forever. And himself, riding among the whites, looking like a white. Perhaps even beginning to feel like a white man? He hoped not. Not completely, anyway. Maybe just enough to take the good parts of that life, and mix it with the good parts of Oglala life. But . . . foolishness. All that had made the Oglala into what they were was now gone . . . their freedom, their liberty to roam their vast ranges, their connection to the land . . . shattered.

But Mary was speaking again. "You said your wife and mother were killed. Was it . . . a raid?"

Gabe smiled. He hoped she could not see the bitterness of the smile. "A raid?" he replied softly. "No . . . something bigger than that. You are thinking of Indians, attacking a wagon train, or a settler's house. It was not like that. We were all in an Arapaho camp. A big camp. The soldiers attacked at dawn, while the People were still sleeping. They had howitzers. I remember a woman carrying half of her baby. The baby had no legs, and its guts were hanging out. It was still living, whimpering, wondering what had happened to it. The soldiers killed men, women, children. The old. Then, when they could not reach the survivors, they gathered all the People's belongings into one place. Everything . . . their lodges, their winter food supply, their clothing, they destroyed everything. Burnt it. So that the People would perish during the wintertime. So that they would be exterminated. They killed my wife and mother. Shot my wife through the belly and head. Ran my mother through with a saber. And she was white. Had blonde hair. But she was with Indians. How did Colonel Chivington put it, after he massacred so many women and children at Sand Creek? 'Nits make lice.' "

Gabe pointed to the old scars. "That's why I made these cuts on my arms and chest. I made them because of my grief over the death of my wife and mother. Over the death of the People."

Gabe abruptly stopped speaking. He had seen the growing horror on the faces of both Mary and Becky. Why had he said so much? Perhaps he was simply weak from his wound.

Mary was silent a moment. Then she stirred herself into action. "Becky," she said, "I think our guest is strong enough to eat something. Could you bring a bowl of soup?"

The girl jumped a little, as if she'd been awakened from a dream. She abruptly stood up and headed out the door. Gabe watched her go, and as she left the room, he realized once again that, from the back, she looked even more like Yellow Buckskin Girl than she did from the front. But this time he did not find the thought disturbing.

Mary saw him looking after the girl. "She's my younger sister. When Mom and Dad died we had her come out here to live with us." She snorted angrily, looking around at the shabby room. "We were living a lot better then."

Becky was back in a few minutes with a shallow bowl of soup. Steam rose from the bowl. Gabe felt his stomach tighten. He remembered the big skin pot of soup always simmering away over the fire inside his mother's lodge. For just a moment the smell of the soup brought along with it other smells: curing hides, the fire in the middle of the lodge, the grease the People used on their hair, the smell of thick buffalo robes, and outside, the smell of the prairie.

It was Becky who fed him the soup. Mary had reached out for it, but Becky had simply sat down on the edge of the bed and presented him with a spoon half full of steaming soup.

Gabe was surprised how difficult eating was. He was still much weaker than he'd thought he was when he'd awakened. He was chagrined to discover that he could only eat a few spoonfuls of the soup.

Becky's face, not far from his own, was quite animated as she fed him. He realized again how lovely she was. "We don't know your name," she blurted.

"Gabe. Gabe Conrad."

"Well . . . I was sure scared, Mr. Conrad, when I found you laying in that big pool of blood, by the spring."

"Afraid I'd get blood in the water?" Gabe asked, smiling a little. "And the name's Gabe."

She appeared flustered. "Oh, no! I . . . well . . . you know. It was kind of a shock."

"I'll bet."

As close as Gabe could guess, he'd put the girl in her late teens. He doubted she was twenty. That was part of it . . . she was close to Yellow Buckskin Girl's age, when she . . .

No. Let that thought go. Forget it for now. The man who'd killed her, Captain Stanley Price, who'd also been the soldier who'd run his sword through the body of Gabe's mother, was long dead. And he'd died hard. Gabe had seen to that. Old stories. All old stories. And now he was faced with a new generation, this girl, and it made him glad to realize that at least one young woman was alive who looked like Yellow Buckskin Girl. In this small way, the world had renewed itself.

It was beginning to be difficult for Gabe to think. And to keep his eyes open. He was very tired. "I think I'm going to sleep a little again," he murmured to the two women.

"Sleep all you can, Mr. Conrad," Mary replied quietly. "You'll get well all that much quicker."

"Please . . . not Mr. Conrad. Call me Gabe," he muttered. Then fell asleep.

This time, when Gabe awoke, it was from a pleasant dream. He felt warm, secure. And sexually excited.

He did not immediately open his eyes. He felt a warm, damp softness against his lower chest. He opened his eyes a crack. The girl, Becky, was washing him. These Jackson women seemed to be fascinated by cleanliness.

Or perhaps that was not what Becky was fascinated by. To wash him, Becky had slid the sheet quite low, baring his penis. As she slowly worked the cloth over his stomach, she was looking lower, at the soft, flaccid mass between Gabe's legs.

Except that it was not quite so soft anymore. Gabe felt slightly alarmed as he began to get an erection. But not too alarmed. For just a little while he put the white man's ways from his mind, their strange sense of shame concerning their bodies. It was so pleasant, what the girl was doing for him. And, looking from beneath his lashes at her dark beauty, he could not help thinking other pleasant thoughts.

The girl's hand holding the washcloth froze on his belly. She was staring hard at his crotch now, mesmerized. His erection rose higher and higher. She did not seem to be breathing.

Gabe sensed when the girl's head began to turn, to look into his face. He quickly closed his eyes, then stirred. He immediately felt the sheet slide higher, covering his crotch. When he opened his eyes, Becky was looking at him fixedly. He noticed that her cheeks were flushed. She was breathing in quick little gasps. "Are . . . are you feeling any better?" she asked in a choked voice.

Gabe drew up his legs so that the drape in the sheet hid his erection. "A lot better now," he murmured. Then he smiled at the girl. She blushed, not knowing just how he had meant the words, how long he'd been awake.

She abruptly stood up. "I'll go get Mary," she said, her voice tight.

"No. Sit here for a while," Gabe replied, patting the side of the bed.

The girl hesitated. Finally, she pulled a straight-backed chair close to the bed and sat, stiffly, about three feet from him. She did not seem to be able to speak at first, but then he noticed that she was looking at his right hand, at the old puncture scar that went all the way through the palm and out the back, and at the broken index finger, with its first joint bent sharply away from the other fingers. "You . . . you sure got a lot of hurts," she said.

"The hand?" he said, raising it. "Another gift from the army. When I was only about nineteen, I was attacked by an army officer. In a barn. He and some of his fellow officers and gentlemen surrounded me, made sure I was not armed. Then this officer tried to kill me with a pitchfork. One of the tines went through my hand while I was taking the pitchfork away from him. The finger? I broke it on his jaw, because the pitchfork wound wouldn't let me close my fist tightly enough."

"But . . . surely it could have been set. The finger, I mean."

Gabe shrugged. "No time for that. I had to run for my life after that. With an old friend. Well, a man who was almost like a father to me. Jim Bridger. Ever hear of him?"

The girl's eyes widened. "Of course! Why, he must be just about the most famous mountain man and Indian scout who ever lived."

Gabe smiled. "Just about. He gave me one of my rifles. The Sharps."

"Really?"

Gabe did not mention that he'd had the fight after getting out of the guardhouse at a military post. He'd spent three years locked in a cell, for an earlier fight he'd had with the same officer. In that fight Gabe had pinned the man's hand to the ground with another pitchfork, when the officer had tried to shoot him. He didn't mention that he'd been at the post because Jim Bridger had kidnapped him from his mother's lodge when he was only a boy of fifteen. With his mother's aid. She had wanted him to go live among the whites, before he got himself killed fighting with the People against the soldiers.

"This army officer," Becky said, "he sounds like a bad man."

"He was," Gabe said woodenly. "He was the same man who killed my wife and my mother."

"Oh, my God!" Becky murmured. "Where . . . where is he now?"

Gabe fell silent as he thought about Captain Stanley Price. His enemy. The man he should have killed the first time he had the chance. "He died a long time ago," Gabe said curtly.

He remembered the burning barn, Price running out into the night, screaming in agony. Gabe had watched him die, his charring body melting and dirtying the crisp white snow that surrounded them. But Price's death had not brought back Yellow Buckskin Girl. Nor had it brought back Amelia Conrad, Gabe's mother.

Becky was speaking again, but he hadn't heard the words. "What?" he asked.

"I said, you must have had a terribly hard life."

Gabe laughed gently. "Better than most of the people I grew up with. I'm still alive."

There was a sound by the door. Gabe looked up and saw Mary and Hal Jackson standing in the doorway. Gabe moved his legs slightly beneath the sheet. Good . . . his erection was gone. He smiled at the Jacksons. Becky saw where he was looking, and she turned. "Oh," she said. "Mr. Conrad . . . Gabe, was telling me the most interesting things. Did you know that Jim Bridger was his father?"

"I said he was almost like a father to me," Gabe corrected.

"You're sure looking stronger," Mary said, coming into the room, with Hal following a step behind. They too pulled up chairs and sat near the bed. "Glad to see you're mending," Hal said quietly.

Gabe could sense the tension, the questions begging to be asked. He decided to anticipate them. "You're wondering what I was doing lying there with a bullet in my hide," he said.

"More or less," Hal replied guardedly.

"The sheriff shot me. He and his cronies robbed me, threw me on a chain gang, then he shot me when I was getting away."

It was out. He watched Hal and Mary Jackson's faces closely. To his surprise, he saw a look of relief come over their features. "We figured it might be something like that," Hal finally said. "We thought you might have run afoul of our beloved sheriff. A lot of men do."

"He's not liked, then."

"Not by us!" Hal said bitterly. "Not by most other people in this county, either. He steals, he cheats, and he kills. Cheated us. We had a big spread right in the center of a beautiful valley. Lots of water and grass, but he took it from us. Phonied up some unpaid tax bills, and confiscated the whole mess. Why do you think we're living in this shack?"

Gabe relaxed a little. He'd fallen among the right people . . . other victims of Sheriff Cleary. "I killed some
men before I got shot. I want you to know that. I must
be a very wanted man."

"Who?" Mary Jackson asked.

"The bartender in town. The one who drugged me.
And some men who worked with him. . . . "

"You killed Josh Peters?" Mary burst out. "My God,
I'm so glad! That sneaking, thieving, murderous little
bastard. . . . "

"And a chain gang guard called Bull. And a deputy
named Buck."

"My God, you have been busy," Hal said in awe.

"Too busy. They'll want me badly. You could get in
a lot of trouble. I should leave here as soon as I can
stand up."

"No! We won't hear of it!" Mary argued. "You'll
leave when you're good and strong. Damn it all, you
don't have to leave at all! We need men like you around
these parts. We need men who will stand up to the likes
of John Cleary and those vultures he has working for
him. We—"

"Wait. Wait a moment," Gabe interrupted. "You're
talking about the county sheriff. An elected official. You
make it sound as if everybody hates him. If they do, why
don't they just vote him out of office?"

Hal smiled bitterly. "They would . . . if they could
get anybody to run against him. A couple of men have
tried. They've had . . . accidents, just before the election. In an area as isolated as this one, once a man gets
power, it's easy to hang on to that power. Especially if
the man's as ruthless as John Cleary."

"Don't forget Lew Duval," Mary broke in. "Sometimes I think he's more crooked than Cleary. Sometimes
I think he's the one who really runs the whole show."

It was as if a dam had burst. Hal and Mary, even
Becky, recited a long list of crimes attributed to the
sheriff, and to a local rancher named Duval. "Duval
has the biggest spread in the whole area," Mary said.
"What Cleary confiscates, Duval picks up for a song.
That includes our land, too. Belongs to Duval now."

They told how Duval stole horses from out of the area, then, with Cleary's help, established false ownership and sold them for a big profit. They detailed how Cleary and Duval worked hand in hand, running a flourishing criminal empire. And no one seemed able to stop them. Anyone opening his or her mouth might be beaten, then run out of the area. People who were a dangerous threat to Duval and Cleary's illegal enterprises usually ended up dead.

"Duval showed up here in the county about five years ago," Hal said. "Got himself a little spread, which grew and grew. Everybody knew he was rustling stock somewhere else to build up his own herds. Nothing was done about it, though. The sheriff we had then was old and worn out. Just didn't care much about anything. When Cleary ran, we all had high hopes about him. He was young, active, full of energy—"

"And he could talk a smooth line," Mary cut in. "He really fooled us. We figure now that Duval provided the money that backed Cleary's run for sheriff. There's talk that they used to be friends somewhere back East. They sure work hand in glove now."

Gabe said nothing. It was the same old story. Greed and corruption. He had little respect for the white man's law. For years the entire country had been run by an unending string of Republican politicians who, after the death of their founding president, Abraham Lincoln, had seemed to believe the nation belonged to them personally. And to the rich men, the industrialists and the big ranchers, the fat cats who backed them for office.

Greed again. The white man's disease. More, always wanting more than they already had, gouging, plotting, scrabbling. It was greed for gold that had caused Gabe's parents, Adam and Amelia Conrad, to branch off the main trail, along with a number of other gold-crazy settlers. Unthinking greed that lured them into the Black Hills, an area sacred to the Lakota and the Cheyenne. It was a band of Oglala Bad Faces who had killed everyone in the party . . . except Amelia Conrad. And the baby she was carrying. Only a few minutes before the attack, she and Adam, full of excitement over their proposed riches, had made passionate love in their wagon. Perhaps it had been that extra excitement that had gotten Amelia pregnant.

She'd been spared, to become the woman of an Oglala warrior, Little Wound, who'd been impressed by her courage during the fight. Gabe had been born among the Oglala. For his first fourteen years he'd been raised like any other Oglala boy. His earliest values had been Lakota values. Values he still admired. Among the People it was considered a mark of honor to be poor, to be the finest hunter and warrior, to give what you had to those less able or less fortunate. To share.

Of course, how much could a nomad carry? Too many possessions meant hardship. Maybe that was the white man's curse: to live in houses that never moved, the way an Oglala lodge moved. A house they could fill up with more things than any person would ever need.

"Greed. . . . "

Gabe picked the word out of something Mary was talking about. Cleary and Duval. "How could they do all those things to people, good people, just for money?" she continued. "I don't understand."

Gabe looked into Mary's honest, pretty face. He felt a surge of warmth for her, for her husband, her sister. They'd taken him in without question, not knowing who or what he might be, knowing only that he was a fellow human being who needed help. They'd cared for him with no expectation of reward. They were the kind of people who became disturbed by the greed of others.

"You're right," he said to Mary. "I don't understand why they would do that either."

He fell silent a moment, his face thoughtful. Then he added, "I suppose they will have to be stopped."

CHAPTER EIGHT

Gabe stood on the rickety porch, enjoying the feel of the sun striking his body. It was his fifth day out of bed, and except for stiffness in his wounded shoulder, he felt he had most of his strength back.

He felt a finger poke at his ribs, low on the right side. He turned quickly, which made his shoulder hurt, then saw that it was only Becky. "Scared you a little bit, didn't I?" she said, grinning.

But she'd seen the slight wince when he turned. "Oh, stupid me. I've hurt your shoulder. Come on . . . come on into the house, and I'll rub on some of that salve Mary makes. You know, the smelly stuff."

Gabe was standing just a couple of feet from the girl. He looked down into her face, struck again by her loveliness. Perhaps some men wouldn't think her beautiful, they might consider her too rustic, with her deep tan and the lack of any attempts to beautify herself with artificial aids, such as creams or rouge. But that was one of the things he liked about her, the naturalness of her beauty.

Other men might not like the way she dressed, either. With work to do around the Jackson's little spread, the girl usually wore a somewhat oversized man's shirt, probably one of Hal's. And she wore jeans. No frilly dresses. Gabe liked the jeans; they emphasized the taut swell of the girl's buttocks. As for the shirt, Becky seemed careless about the buttons, often leaving the top two or three undone. Because the shirt was so big, it sometimes gaped open, giving him a view of high, round breasts. Quite large breasts.

He was beginning to wonder if these glimpses were as ingenuous as they seemed. Were they merely innocent accidents on the part of a young woman who had been around too few men? Or were they calculated? Perhaps the girl had an instinctive knowledge of how to use her beauty, already understood the power that glimpses of that lovely young body would have over a man.

She'd been dancing around Gabe like a puppy ever since he'd stopped being bedridden. "Let the man have some peace," Hal had told her once.

"Uh-uh," Becky had replied artlessly. "He's mine. I found him."

Yes, there was that about her behavior, a proprietary gleam in her eyes. Gabe was her pet, and she was damned well going to play with him.

But . . . play in what way? Several times, when Becky had not been aware that Gabe was watching her out of the corners of his eyes, he'd seen a peculiar look come over the girl's face as she stared at him. It took him a couple of days to identify that look: lust, mixed with fear. Maybe she'd spent too much time bathing his naked body. Gabe remembered the occasion when he'd gotten the erection, remembered the fascination on the girl's face.

He put the thought from his mind. Becky was the younger sister of the woman who had taken the bullet out of his shoulder. The woman who, with her ointments and her knowledge of frontier medicine, had probably saved his life. Damned if he'd offend his hosts by taking advantage of Mary's little sister . . . even if she was so obviously ripe, so ready and willing to be taken advantage of.

Becky pulled him into the house. "You sit here," she said, plunking him down onto a chair. He heard her rummaging around through a cupboard. She came back with a tin of Mary's ointment. "You'll smell a little funny, but it'll loosen up the muscles," she said. She was trying to appear businesslike but he could detect an underlying tension in her voice.

Her fingers were busy with his shirt buttons, racing, even fumbling a little. She peeled the shirt down around his waist, then stood for a moment, studying his well-muscled chest and shoulders. With a little shudder, she turned her gaze away, then pried the top off the tin.

She was right, the stuff did smell. But it was also very effective. As Becky massaged the salve into his skin, the muscles beneath began to unknot. Her fingers were soothing. Despite her healthy strength, she had a delicate touch.

Gabe turned to thank the girl. She was standing beside him, bending down a little as she stroked lotion into the skin of his middle back. When he turned, their faces were only a few inches apart. He found himself looking straight into Becky's huge brown eyes. He noticed how creamy the skin of her face was, admired the apparent softness of her mouth. Oh, God, he thought, trapped by the girl's eyes, by the promise shining within them. One of her breasts was brushing his shoulder. He could feel its firm resiliency, its feminine softness. Oh, God, he thought again. I'm lost.

Because she wanted him. He could sense it, see it, feel it, even smell it, smell the musky scent of a woman's arousal. The scent of a sexually excited woman, coming from this girl.

He almost reached out for her, almost swept her into his arms, but managed to hold himself back. Rigidly. Becky seemed to realize it. She stepped away from him, banged the lid into place.

When he turned, she was looking straight at him, the tin of salve clutched in both hands. "Hal thinks I'm just a little kid, you know. Still a little kid. But I'll be nineteen next month. That's not so little. Mary understands. She knows."

She turned away, and began to return the salve to its cupboard. Gabe sat, staring at her lithe back, the round swell of her hips. No telling what might have happened between them if Mary's voice hadn't come singing from the kitchen. "Lunch, everybody. Come and get it, or I'll feed it to the hogs."

That's what Mary always said when a meal was ready. Although there was only one hog, and she'd die before she gave it anything but scraps.

Gabe stood up and put on his shirt. He had a little trouble getting his left arm into the sleeve. "Here . . . let me help," Becky said. She smoothed the shirt into place, then began to button it. She was standing right in front of Gabe, with the top of her head level with his mouth. He stared at the part of her hair, at the smooth skin beneath. Her forehead curved away, with those marvelous eyes just below. She fastened the last button, then looked up. She gave a little start when she realized he was looking straight down at her, and for just a moment a flash of adolescent fear flickered over her face. Fear of the unknown.

Flustered, the girl moved away. "We better go eat," she murmured. "You know how Mary carries on if we let it get cold."

As she headed toward the door, Gabe thought he heard her mutter, half under her breath, "Almost nineteen."

The four of them sat around the pine table. As usual, the meal was mostly beef. Hal made no bones about the fact that he occasionally shot one of Lew Duval's cows. "They rightly belong to me, anyhow," he'd mutter.

Gabe enjoyed these meals; there was a lot of family warmth around the cracked and leaning table. At times he was reminded of the warmth inside his mother's lodge. What was lacking here was the warmth of a whole people being together, the sounds of a village outside, teaming with life. How strange that so many whites tended to live alone, in little family groups. As if they did not need one another. As if they did not need community warmth.

Gabe detected tension today. Hal wrinkled his nose. "What's that smell?" he asked.

"Oh," Becky said nonchalantly, "I put some of Mary's salve on Gabe's shoulder."

"I see," Hal said shortly, almost grunted it.

"It's amazing how quickly Gabe heals," Mary put in.

"He'll be right as rain in no time."

She looked at Gabe a little wistfully. "I guess you'll be riding right out of our lives, then."

"I suppose I'll be riding somewhere," Gabe replied, feeling a little uncomfortable, shamed by the stricken look on Becky's face.

The meal seemed to go on for a long time. Finally, Becky excused herself and left the table. Gabe found he had little appetite. He too got up and left. "I think I'll take a walk . . . get some exercise."

Hal and Mary watched him go out the door. "He's kind of impressive, isn't he?" Mary said to Hal once Gabe was out of hearing.

Hal nodded glumly. "Maybe too impressive. Have you seen the way Becky looks at him? And why the hell was she putting that salve on him? You should be doing that kind of thing, Mary."

Mary grinned mischievously. "Are you so anxious to get rid of me?"

Hal flushed. "Of course not. . . . Oh, I see what you mean. Yes, he's a really good-looking man. Which is why I don't like the idea of Becky hanging around him so much. She's no kid anymore. . . . "

"Exactly," Mary cut in. Her voice had a sharpness that surprised Hal. "She's no kid. She's almost nineteen. Don't forget that we were married when I was still seventeen."

"What? Married? You're thinking that about them, Mary? Well . . . that's not likely to happen. That man's a wanderer. I know one when I see one. Not that I hold it against him. What's more likely to happen, with Becky having all those stars in her eyes, is something a lot more simple."

"Good," Mary replied tartly. "She needs some experience. And if that experience ties Gabe a little more tightly to this place, for even a few weeks, things might happen. To Cleary. You saw the look in his eyes when we told him about Cleary and Duval. He's the kind of man who'd go right after them."

Hal's mouth was hanging open. "You'd be willing to trade your sister, I mean, her virtue, so we could hang on to a man who's good with a gun?"

"I'd be willing to do a lot to get back what's ours," she snapped. Then her voice softened. "What's all this talk about selling my sister's virtue? You men. You're the ones who made up this virtue, this virginity thing . . . so you could hang on to us, make us belong to you. I want the girl to have experience, to know a little about men, so that she doesn't get all frustrated someday and marry the first halfway good-looking man who comes along. I want her to have known at least one good man, so she can make a decent choice. And I happen to think that Gabe, despite the way he grew up, or maybe even because of it, is a good man. An honest man, who won't just use a girl then make her feel like garbage when he throws her away. You're probably right, I think he'll leave someday, there's that in him. But I don't think he'll make Becky feel like garbage. So there!"

Hal was staring strangely at his wife. "I never knew you felt like this, Mary." A note of bitterness crept into his voice. "Maybe you'd have liked that experience, too. Maybe . . . "

Mary laughed, a warm, affectionate laugh. She lay her hand on her husband's arm. "I didn't need it, Hal. I got lucky, first thing, when I met you. But I can't be sure Becky will be so lucky. You're one of a kind."

Mollified, but perhaps wondering if his wife knew more about managing him than he'd ever imagined, Hal got to his feet. "Well," he muttered, "doesn't sound right to me, but she's your sister. Ah, hell, think I'll go do some work."

Mary stood up with him. "To hell with the work. They're gone . . . outside. The house is ours. Why don't we just . . . go into our room. The two of us . . . alone."

Hal felt a slow heat building inside his body. Damned if he didn't have the most amazing wife. Most women would have waited for some advance from her husband. Not Mary. She too was one of a kind. "Yeah," he said, somewhat thickly, sliding his arm around Mary's waist, alive to the soft strength of her. A beautiful woman. "To hell with the work."

But as both walked into their bedroom, neither could help images forming in their minds. Images of Gabe and Becky, and what they might be doing.

Those were exactly the kind of images Gabe was trying to put out of his mind. He'd sensed the tension at the table; the Jacksons knew what was going on. Or maybe they only thought they did. Hell, he didn't know himself!

He was out of sight of the house now, walking through a grove of cottonwoods. He realized he was headed toward the spring.

He suddenly caught sight of movement near some bushes to his right. Becky. She walked onto the path, hands in the pockets of her jeans, head down a little. "Guess we're going in the same direction," she murmured, looking a little hangdog.

"I guess so."

She looked up, shoulders hunched. "Mind if I walk along with you?"

Becky looked so young, so hopeful. Gabe felt a surge of warmth toward the girl, toward her basic humanity. Armed with this sudden sense of virtue, he smiled. "Sure. I'd like that."

He was rewarded by a radiant smile. "Great!" she said. "Hey . . . let's go look at where I found you."

They walked toward the spring, Becky chattering gaily. Gabe envied the girl; it sure didn't take much to make her happy. They reached the spot where he'd fallen from his horse. The place looked quite natural now, but when Becky scuffed at the ground with the toe of her shoe, the earth beneath was dark and crusted . . . with blood. "Yuk!" she mouthed.

She looked up at Gabe. "I don't think I want to be in this place," she said abruptly. "Let's walk down to the pond."

The girl's somber mood only lasted until they were out of sight of the spring. She was literally skipping along, which Gabe liked; her breasts were bouncing playfully inside her shirt.

Becky's mood grew even more exuberant when they reached the pond. The runoff from the spring, having

reached a pocket in the earth, formed a deep, placid
pool, ringed by a profusion of plant life. There was
animal life, too. As they approached, a huge bullfrog
plopped into the water.

"Let's go for a swim!" Becky burst out. "It's so hot,
and the water looks so nice. . . . "

Yes, it was hot. Gabe's wound had closed, perhaps the
water would be soothing. To swim a little, to exercise his
shoulder with the support of the water . . .

However, there were the usual proprieties among the
whites. "I don't know," he said dutifully.

"Oh!" Becky said disgustedly. "You're such an old
stick in the mud. Well, even if you aren't going swim-
ming, I am!"

The girl strode purposefully toward a clump of bushes
right at the water's edge. Gabe watched her go, smiling
a little. He liked her independence, her willingness to
stick her neck out.

"Don't you peek!" she called from behind the bush,
which, of course, only makes a person look all the harder. Gabe saw the girl's shirt sail through the air and drape
itself over part of the bush. He heard rustlings of cloth,
and knew that the jeans would soon follow.

Becky had chosen a rather thin bush. Gabe caught
glimpses of shining flesh, the roundness of a breast.
Then, with a whoop, Becky launched her naked body
into the water, in a rather clumsy dive, just a flash of
bare flesh, then a big gout of water, and the girl's body
disappeared beneath the surface.

Gabe saw her head pop up near the middle of the pond.
"Oh, it feels so good," Becky called out. "Come on . . .
jump in."

Why not? Gabe thought. He started toward the bush
where Becky had undressed. "What's the matter? Are
you afraid I'll see you naked?" Becky chided. "I've been
washing you for days, Gabe."

So she had. Gabe stood at the edge of the pond
and stripped off his clothes. Becky was quite silent
now, watching him. Apparently, washing his unconscious body was quite a different thing from watching
him strip naked out in the open.

Gabe entered the water in a long, flat dive. His momentum took him close to Becky. She had floated higher in the water. He could see the shadowy shape of her breasts just beneath the surface. They were large, full breasts, perfectly formed. The coolness of the water had puckered the nipples a little.

Becky saw where he was looking, and smiled. "Race you to the bottom," she said. The girl twisted in the water, upending herself. For a couple of seconds her buttocks were clear of the surface, taut, sleek globes. He caught a glimpse of dark fur between her thighs, then the entire enchanting picture disappeared beneath the water.

Gabe followed the girl, diving deep. Once beneath the reflective sheet of the pond's surface, the water was fairly clear. Eyes open, he watched Becky swim hard for the sandy bottom. Her body shimmered, its form distorted by the water's refractive qualities. Lovely.

She saw him following her, and twisted to the side, breaking for the surface again. They came up close together. Laughing, Becky splashed water in his face. "Isn't this wonderful!" she burst out. "I've never had anybody to swim with before."

For the next five minutes Becky played like a puppy, cavorting in the water, splashing Gabe, once diving below him, seizing his leg, dragging him under. He wrestled with her beneath the water, breaking free, conscious of the resilient softness of her naked body.

"Bet you can't catch me," Becky called out. She swam toward the bank, Gabe after her. He knew he couldn't catch the girl; she swam like a fish, and his shoulder was still a little weak. However, she let herself get trapped against the bank. She tried to slip past him, laughing happily, but she was in a miniature cove, and he reached out and took hold of her.

Their feet were on the bottom. The water was not so deep here, coming to just below the girl's breasts. She tried to struggle free, laughing.

Then the game suddenly became much more serious. Gabe was holding the girl in a tight grasp. Her breasts were pressing against his lower chest. He could feel her legs rubbing against his own. Her thighs parted as she struggled, and he felt the softness of her pubic hair pressing against his leg. This is getting dangerous, he thought. But he did not release her.

Suddenly Becky stopped struggling. He looked down into her face, saw that she was looking back up at him, her expression no longer laughing and carefree, but sultry, her eyes huge, darkening with the beginnings of passion.

Gabe realized he was getting an erection. So did Becky; she could feel it pressing against the lower part of her belly. "Oh, my God," she murmured, then ground her body hard against him.

The rest was simply a process of following nature; there was no way either of them could change what was about to happen. It was simply instinct. One of Becky's legs rose, locking around Gabe's waist, while her hips churned against his body. He raised her higher against him; it was easy because of the water. Their lips met in a wild, fumbling kiss, teeth clashing, their breath panting into each other's mouths.

Then he was in her. "Ah!" Becky cried out. She arched, her upper body leaning away from his chest, but now she had raised her other leg, and had both of them wrapped around his waist, pulling her groin tightly against his own, so that they were anchored together.

Gabe felt the girl shudder. He shuddered too, overcome by the pleasure of having her envelope him. They stayed locked together for only a little while, then Gabe, who had not had a woman for some time, who had certainly not had one quite like Becky, felt the semen rushing out of him, into the girl's vagina. She shuddered once again, then suddenly went limp, sliding away from him.

He had to support her; her legs seemed unable to do the job. And she was sobbing quietly. A little concerned, he helped her onto shore, leading her to a grassy place where they could both lie down. She lay on her back, arms outspread, breasts pulled high, breathing heavily.

It was then that he noticed thin streaks of blood on her thighs, mixed with the water that was still draining from her skin. A virgin. As he'd suspected, she'd been a virgin.

Was he in big trouble now? Would she run, screaming, to her sister and her brother-in-law, shouting rape?

"I'm . . . I'm sorry. . . . " he began to say.

The girl's eyes flew open. "Sorry?" she burst out. "Whatever for?"

"But . . . you're crying."

"Of course I'm crying, you ninnie! It was so wonderful! It was . . . incredible!"

"It . . . didn't hurt?"

She nodded vigorously. "Sure. But I knew about that. Mary told me once that it hurt a lot the first time. But, what I didn't expect is that the rest of it would feel so darned *good*."

They lay silently for a while. "I was kinda scared at first, though," Becky finally admitted. "When I knew it was finally going to happen. I . . . just couldn't seem to stop myself, it *had* to happen."

She looked over at Gabe questioningly. "Didn't it?"

He nodded. "Nature has put some strong urges into us. That's how we make more people."

Becky looked disappointed. "Is that all it was? Just nature? You didn't . . . like me for myself?"

Oops. Gabe caught himself, enmeshed now in womankind's endless struggle to weld a mate to her . . . permanently. He turned his head and smiled at the girl. "You're a wonderful person, Becky."

He meant it. She was not only beautiful, but courageous, full of life and laughter, and now, as he'd just discovered, full of passion.

"Guess I am a woman now. A real woman," the girl said, just a little smugly. He could read the triumph on her face, not triumph over him, but triumph over something her body had been urging her toward for a long time. The fear and uncertainty were gone for her now, replaced by a sense of accomplishment, of having arrived.

He was impressed, a feeling he seldom had toward white women. Most of the ones he'd met had been so repressed, physically and mentally, by their rigid, prudish society, that they were more trouble than they were worth. Becky, on the other hand, seemed quite eager to enjoy her body's pleasures. Perhaps she was simply too young to have acquired the normal load of shame and guilt. Perhaps it was living out here, isolated, away from society. Or perhaps it was the influence of her older sister. Mary was an impressive woman, apparently free of many of the restraints that shackled other white women.

He was looking at the girl's body. A definitely pleasurable occupation. He noticed something. "You're tan all over," he observed.

She grinned like a satisfied cat. "I spend a lot of time lying here in the sun. Nobody ever bothers me."

"Lucky sun, to have spent so many hours with your beautiful body."

She arched her back involuntarily, pleased by his compliment. Her breasts thrust skyward. "You really think I'm beautiful?"

She asked it with such innocent wonder that Gabe could not help but feel a surge of warmth. "All of you is beautiful," he replied. "This part . . . and this part, and . . . all the rest."

His hands began to rove over her flesh, his palm stroking her breasts, teasing her nipples into an involuntary hardness. He played with these soft little buds until the girl began to wriggle with pleasure.

His hands roamed lower, his fingertips brushing through the soft damp hair between her legs. When he pressed down on the vulva beneath, the girl let out a sharp gasp.

"Did that hurt?" he asked.

She shook her head wildly. "Uh-uh. It . . . it feels . . . wonderful."

Gabe was getting another erection. Becky felt it against her thigh. "Oh, let me see, let me touch it, let me feel it."

Her fingers gently stroked the length of his erection, then closed around it firmly. "Oh! It's so *hard!*" she blurted.

"All the better to make love to you with," Gabe said thickly.

"Again? You're going to do it to me again?"

There was no mistaking the enthusiasm in her voice. Gabe rolled on top of her, parted her vaginal lips with the head of his penis, and slowly entered. He felt her flinch from the pain of her ruptured hymen, but once he was all the way in, he was welcomed once again by that involuntary shudder. "Oh, God," she murmured over and over again, as her legs rose to tighten around his hips. Her own hips began to buck uncontrollably, and for the next few minutes Gabe had a hard ride.

Later, they lay side by side again. Becky gazed dreamily up at the bright blue sky. "I can't believe it," she murmured, her fingers trailing over Gabe's sweat-slick belly. "I can't believe anything could feel so wonderful. It's . . . It's . . . oh, there aren't any words for it. Are there?"

"Nope."

Eventually it was time to go back to the house . . . before search parties were sent out, to find them lying together naked. Reluctantly, they got up and dressed, Becky just a little bashful now as she pulled on her clothes. They walked back to the house in silence. Gabe was worried. Anybody with any brains could take a look at them and know what had happened. Becky had that soft, langourous, satisfied, almost sleepy air of a woman who has just been made love to. They'd know.

They did. Both Hal and Mary. It was in their eyes as Gabe and Becky walked toward the porch. Gabe sensed Becky stiffen with anticipation of a very bad time ahead.

Then Gabe noticed something about Mary. She too had that soft, langourous, almost sleepy air. She looked from Becky back to Gabe, her eyes full of awareness.

Then she smiled, a warm, happy smile. And Gabe knew that it was going to be all right.

CHAPTER NINE

Over millennia, the rain, the wind, and the sun had formed a natural seat out of the stone, sculpted it right at the edge of a cliff. Gabe sat in this stone seat, with empty space falling away beneath his feet. This was his watching place. This was the kind of place he'd hoped to find in the mountains, a vantage point from which he could survey a great sweep of land.

He sat surrounded by brush, but the brush was thin enough so that he could see through it. He studied the terrain below, partly to look for danger, partly for the sheer beauty of the view. The mountains swept away below him, down toward the plain. Here, there was pine and thick green undergrowth, below, the dun-colored plain, streaked with a lighter, less substantial green. Far away, to the west, the horizon was lost in a thin blue haze as the sun sucked water from the soil.

He'd been coming to this place for a week. When he'd asked Becky if there were any good vantage points close by, she had led him to this one. She knew this country as if it were part of her own body.

The girl's body. Several times she had come here with him. He'd finally decided that her presence definitely distracted his attention. The girl had a tendency to take her clothes off at the slightest provocation. Having her

lying next to him, with the sun lighting up her golden
flesh, was, to say least, very distracting. He had usually not been able to resist the urge to make love to the
girl, as was, of course, the reason she was lying there
naked.

Like most young women who had just had a recent
and satisfying introduction to sex, Becky had quickly
grown insatiable. Night and day her body shuddered,
burned, and ached with desire. Gabe had been happy
enough to ease her suffering . . . within the confines of
good taste. Although Hal and Mary were not making any
complaints, Gabe had no desire to wave his and Becky's
sexual activities in their faces.

Most of their lovemaking had been outdoors. A lot
of it right here. There was a soft grassy spot about ten
yards back from the edge of the cliff, a little hollow.
The grass was looking just a bit ragged at the moment;
he and Becky had spent many pleasant hours grinding
it into the ground.

As he looked out over the valley, Gabe found his
view obscured by a memory of Becky, a very arrest-
ing memory, a mental image of the girl sitting astride
him. That had become one of her favorite ways of
making love, although she seemed bound and determined to try them all. He particularly liked it when
she straddled him, because then he could look up at her,
watch her breasts jiggle as she writhed above him, her
hands on his chest, her face glowing with passion, her
eyes glittering unseeingly, with all of her attention
focused either inside her, or perhaps in some distant place inaccessible to Gabe. He thought about the
way her mouth would pop open into a little "Oh!" of
delight each time he first entered her, as if it had never
happened before, as if each time were the first amazing moment of something truly incredible, totally unex-
pected.

Gabe was vaguely uneasy. Something had been started
between them when they'd first made love at the pond.
Something powerful. He now had a very strong tie to
this place. He was attracted to the girl, to her innocent
delight in their lovemaking. And attracted just as much to

her personality. Becky was a young woman of courage, stuffed full of life, excitement, a sense of adventure. But damn it, she was so young! And . . . what if she became pregnant?

Gabe felt the light touch of invisible shackles tickling his wrists. Shackles more potent than the ones he'd worn on the chain gang, because he was forging them himself. Part of him wanted to be tied to the girl, to be able to pass his days looking into her huge dark eyes, touching, stroking, making love to her lovely body. He wanted to be fully aware, each day, of her desire for him. And of his desire for her.

His eyes returned to the enormous vista below him. There was that, too. A vast world out there, and all of his instincts drove him to roam over it. To wander. No . . . it was more than instinct, there was also his training, the way he had grown up. The Lakota had been a nomadic people—before they'd been herded onto the reservations. The camp had constantly moved to follow the herds of buffalo on which the People depended for their sustenance. The mighty, numberless buffalo, whose flesh, hide, bones, sinews provided food, shelter, clothing, thread. Even the animals' dried dung provided cooking fuel for the lodges.

Gabe had grown up imbued with a tremendous urge to move on. As a boy he'd loved the excitement of striking camp, watching the lodges coming down, helping—until he got older and his male pride intervened—to fasten the lodge poles behind ponies, to be used as travois, with all the family possessions firmly lashed into place, ready to bump along behind the pack horses.

That was the reason he felt his attachment to Becky as invisible chains, slipping around his wrists. If he had been with the People, he would have welcomed this joining together with the girl. The thought of her becoming pregnant would have overjoyed him. Together, he, the girl, their children, would have roamed with the rest of the tribe over their vast lands.

But that was not the way it was with the whites. A man and a woman were expected to find a home, some small house which, to a man like Gabe, quickly became a prison, a smelly cage that was too rigid, too heavy to pack up and move with him. Worst of all, even if a man found a woman who liked to roam, there was no village, no People, to move along with them, to provide continuity, a sense of group. Tribe. This was a feature of the white man's life Gabe had never grown accustomed to.

Gabe's musing abruptly came to a halt. He was sure he'd seen movement far below. He reached behind him for the binoculars he always brought to this watching place. Settling down on his belly, he slowly swept the binoculars over the terrain below.

Yes. There they were. Men. Somewhere close to a dozen; they were too far away yet to count exactly. Over the next half hour Gabe continued to study the riders below, until he was certain that they were headed his way. The valley up which they were riding would lead them straight to the Jackson place.

A beam of sunlight winked off the front of one of the rider's shirt. A badge. It must be Cleary, or a posse of his men, led by a deputy.

Keeping low, in case the men below also had binoculars, Gabe slipped away from the edge of the cliff. When he was able to stand erect, he ran back toward the house. Mary saw him coming. "What is it?" she asked, her face creasing into a worried frown.

Hal and Becky came out onto the porch. Becky was still pouting a little because Gabe had not taken her with him to his stone chair. Now her face paled when she heard him say, "It's a posse. Heading this way. I have to be gone within fifteen minutes. There must be nothing left to show I was ever here."

Becky let out a little wail of sorrow. Hal looked at her sharply. Mary took the girl's arm. "Stop feeling sorry for yourself and start helping," the older woman said firmly.

Gabe's horse was brought from the corral. He quickly loaded it with all his gear. As he was stuffing the Sharps into its scabbard, he turned to Hal. "When I ride away, take a piece of brush, one with a lot of leaves, and smooth away my tracks."

Hal nodded. The women remained on the porch as Gabe mounted. Becky's little lapse of grief had vanished. She looked quite determined now. "Where'll you go?" she called out to her lover.

"Not far. I'll come back later. I want to find out what they have to say."

That brought a smile to the girl's face. "We'll make them talk," she said gaily. To her this was a lark.

"You won't say a damned thing," Hal snapped. "Let me and Mary do the talking."

Gabe touched his hat and pulled his horse around. As he rode out of the yard, he picked a route that would be easiest for Hal to brush clean of tracks. He looked behind him, seeing that Hal was already doing just that. A moment later he was into light timber, out of sight of the house.

He had already picked a good hiding spot, about a quarter of a mile from the house, a little canyon where he could shelter his horse. Even if he was discovered, the canyon mouth was very narrow. He could easily cover it with a rifle, picking off any man foolish enough to enter, and under cover of his fire, ride away up the canyon.

As soon as he reached the canyon he hid his horse behind some boulders. Damned if he'd wait. He pulled both rifles from their saddle scabbards, and loped back toward the house, running silently on moccasined feet.

A small ridge overlooked the house. Gabe headed for it. Even if he were discovered there, any pursuers would have to take a very long way around the ridge. He could escape easily.

He reached the ridge just as a group of a dozen horsemen rode into the yard. Flattening down onto his belly, Gabe saw that the Jackson family had had the sense to pretend to go about their ordinary activities. Becky was just coming back from the henhouse with a basket of eggs. Mary was washing clothes on the front porch. Hal was replacing a cracked pole in the corral.

As the riders came into the yard Hal walked back toward the porch, and his women. The three of them were standing together as the first rider reached the porch. He was the one with the badge. Gabe did not recognize him.

Apparently Hal did. "Rawls," he said. "What the hell are you doing with a badge? Find it somewhere?"

Even from his vantage point, more than a hundred yards away, Gabe could see the man's grin. "Hell, why not a badge? When Buck got hisself killed, Cleary needed another good man. He picked me."

"That would figure," Hal said cryptically.

The smile vanished from Rawls's face. "I hope you don't mean nothin' cute by that," he drawled.

"You can make out of it what you want," Hal replied. "Now . . . what are you doing on my place, scattering horseshit all over the yard?"

One of the riders snickered. Rawls turned in the saddle, pinning the man with his glare. The man stopped snickering.

Rawls turned back toward Hal. "Lookin' for a man. Escaped from the county chain gang. Killed a couple of guards, then came into town and killed a whole bunch more people. Including ol' Buck. We already found some of the other 'scaped prisoners. But not this one. An' Cleary wants him real bad."

"And you're riding out this far?" Hal asked, managing to sound surprised.

"Yeah. No sign of him anywhere else. You seen, heard anything?"

"What would I hear out here, Rawls? Except wind in the trees."

This was said quite bitterly. Rawls grinned again. "Yeah. Ain't quite like the old place, is it? Too bad you didn't pay your taxes."

Hal chose to say nothing. Rawls leaned forward in his saddle. "All of us, Cleary especially, was real surprised to hear that you hadn't left the county. I wouldn't think there'd be anything left here for you, Jackson."

"You're looking at what I got left," Hal said coldly. "And I think I'll keep it. Not even Cleary, or Duval, would want this small a place."

"Don't bet on it, Jackson . . . if you're thinkin' about making any trouble. Now . . . about this fugitive. If you hear or see anything, we want to hear about it, too. Got that? If we figure you're hidin' anything, it'll go hard for you, Jackson. Real hard."

Suddenly Becky spoke up. "Why don't you just ride right on out of our yard, mister, and stop bothering us. Haven't you and your darned crooked bosses caused us enough trouble?"

Rawls slowly turned his head toward the girl. Gabe could only see the man's profile, but he was sure he was grinning. "Well, well," the deputy drawled. "Little Miss Becky. You sure have grown up. Why, you're fair to splitting the seams o' that shirt . . . here and there . . . in all the right places. Bet you'd give a man a real comfortable ride, little lady."

Hal took a step forward, reaching for an ax handle. Rawls saw him coming. A gun suddenly appeared in his hand. He was fast. Gabe quickly took hold of his Sharps, put it to his shoulder. He was careful about cocking it. He held the trigger back as he cranked the big side hammer into position, so that there would be no telltale *clink-clunk* that would give away his position. Only when the hammer was all the way back did he ease the trigger forward, so that its sear caught the hammer slot. Gabe aimed straight at the middle of Rawls's body. At this range he couldn't miss. Not with the Sharps.

But Hal had stopped his forward motion the moment he saw the pistol aimed at him. He moved his hand away from the ax handle. Gabe saw that Mary had him by his other arm, holding him back. "Did you come here to molest young women, Rawls?" Hal asked tightly.

"You shut your face," Rawls snapped. Gabe could see the snarl on the man's face. He shifted the Sharps's sights higher, ready to blast the snarl away in a froth of blood, skin, and bone.

"Oh, hell, Pete," one of the posse members said to Rawls. "We're wastin' our time here. That yahoo we're after probably rode outta the county right after he shot up the town. An' I don't go for hasslin' no women."

He was staring straight at Rawls. He was a big man, tough-looking. Gabe stared hard at his face. Perhaps, when the day comes, Gabe thought, I'll let that one live.

Because he knew he was going to kill these men, all of them if he had to. Rawls for certain. He was tempted to kill Rawls now. But there were too many of them. He'd never get them all before he was forced to run, and then the Jacksons would be in a great deal of trouble. Better to hold his fire now . . . unless Rawls didn't put that pistol away.

Rawls glared at the big man who'd challenged him. The big man glared right back. Rawls's gaze fell away; apparently he had either fear or respect for the other man. The pistol slid back into its holster as smoothly as it had appeared in Rawls's hand. "Yeah . . . guess you're right, Hank. He's long gone. Come on, boys . . . let's ride outta this chicken coop."

The men began pulling their horses around. Gabe took his eyes from the rifle's sights, until he saw Rawls once again turn his horse back to face the trio on the porch. "Don't be surprised if I come a callin', Miss Becky," he drawled, leering. "Time you found out about men."

Then he whirled his horse and rode away after the others. Gabe followed him with the rifle sights, aching to blow him out of the saddle, burning with anger, noticing the way Becky was standing, angry, humiliated.

But Gabe did not fire. Instead, he waited until the men had ridden out of sight and hearing. Only then did he move back away from the edge of the ridge, and head for his horse.

He did not immediately ride back toward the house, but took a circuitous route back to his stone chair. Peering down the valley, he saw that the posse was indeed heading away from the area. They were already about a mile away. Taking out his binoculars, he counted them carefully. Yes. A dozen riders. They had not left anyone behind, to spy on the Jackson place. That was good, because if any of them had come back, there would have been killing. Gabe knew he would not have been able to stop himself.

He turned his horse and rode back toward the house, anger still burning in him over the way Becky had been insulted. This man, this deputy. Rawls. He was going to have to die.

CHAPTER TEN

When Gabe rode into the yard, the look on his face frightened Becky. And excited her, too. She was now seeing a totally new dimension of her gentle lover. The avenger. The killer. She felt a terrible wet warmth between her thighs.

Hal read his face, too. "You heard."

"Yes. I was up on that little ridge. Who is the man, Rawls?"

Hal made a face. "A two-bit gunman who got run out of the county a few years ago by the old sheriff. When Cleary took over, he came back. Cleary didn't have much use for him at first, but I guess he does now, with Buck gone. I almost think I prefer Buck."

Gabe looked straight at Hal. Hal had trouble meeting his eyes. "Rawls will have to die, of course. Even if it's only for what he said to Becky."

This was said in such a matter-of-fact way that Hal flinched a little. He tried to look past the surface of Gabe's eyes, but could not. Gabe's face was totally expressionless.

Becky felt a little scared, wondering where her lover had gone. But the warmth between her thighs was steadily increasing.

Gabe had noticed the reaction of the others. He'd

always been puzzled by the white man's aversion to killing someone who needed killing. Mary was the only one who reacted in a way he could understand. He saw the triumphant gleam in her eyes as she thought about the imminent deaths of her enemies. She would have made a good Oglala woman, a wife for a warrior.

"I'll have to leave here," Gabe continued. "Once the fighting starts, there will be a great deal of trouble. Men will be hunting me everywhere."

"No!" Becky cried out. "You can't leave!"

"She's right," Hal said. "You're welcome here as long as you want to stay. Don't worry about getting us into trouble. We—"

"That's not my only worry," Gabe corrected. "Here, I would be easy to find. Trapped in a box, in one place. Out there . . . " He waved his hand at the vastness of the mountains that surrounded them, the plains below.

"You're bound on riding out, then. You're bound on going after Cleary and his bunch."

"Yes. They've robbed me, imprisoned me, shot me. They've robbed you, also, and now they insult the people who saved my life. I think that is enough reason."

"I suppose so. But, God, man, you can't go after them alone. Wait until you can get some help."

Gabe shook his head. "Right now I think one man alone, one man who knows how to hide, and to strike when he's ready, can do more good than a dozen men. However, I can use what you have in your head. I'd like to hear everything you know about Cleary, and this man Duval, and anyone else who you think is on their side."

"That's easy. And you can ride back in from time to time. I'll start going into town, listening to the latest news. I'll keep you up to date. I'll talk to some other people I know who would like to see Cleary fall. You can count on them for help whenever you need it."

Gabe nodded, then finally dismounted. He and Hal went into the house, where, for the next twenty minutes, they talked. Hal filled him in on Duval's horse-stealing activities. Gabe was very interested. "I think that's where to hit them first."

Finally, it was time to leave. When the two men went outside together, Gabe saw that only Mary was there. "Where's Becky?" Hal asked.

Mary sighed. "She went off in a snit. Doesn't like the idea of Gabe leaving. We've been spoiling her, letting her do whatever she wants . . . "

She suddenly realized what she'd been saying, glanced quickly at Gabe, then actually blushed.

Gabe's face remained expressionless, although he indulged himself in a secret smile. Yes, she'd certainly let her little sister do what she wanted. However, he was sorry that the girl was not here. He would have liked to say good-bye to her.

He mounted his horse. "So long," Hal said, reaching up to shake his hand. "Wish I was going with you."

"That time may come."

He rode out of the yard, then headed along the path that would take him out of the hills, toward the plain below. He felt a slight pang leaving the Jackson place behind him, more for the Jacksons themselves than for the place. And leaving the girl. On the other hand, how wonderful it was to feel free again, on the move, alive, ready to fight. Which was what he had been brought up to do. Fight the enemy. Fight those who attacked the People. Fight those who harmed the weak and helpless. And of course, fight back against those who had harmed him.

He'd read the words in his mother's Bible about turning the other cheek, about forgiving one's enemies, and these ideas had made some inroads on his Oglala upbringing. But more than anything else, he was angry now. Very angry. He remembered the way Rawls had insulted Becky, the insolence of it, his certainty that he would not be called to account for whatever he did. Because he enjoyed the protection of the sheriff, the man who was sworn to uphold the law in this area. That was all the white man had. The law. And when the law itself was subverted . . .

He was suddenly aware of a patch of blue on a bush ahead. He rode closer, cautiously, until he noticed that it was a pair of jeans. My God, they were Becky's jeans;

he could still see the shape of her buttocks in the way they hung from the bush.

What the hell . . . ? Had Rawls come back? No . . . he'd seen the posse riding away down the mountain.

He spotted another flash of color, farther off the trail. Gabe pushed his horse into the brush. It was Becky's shirt. Ten yards from that, a flash of white. Underwear.

Gabe rode past this last flag; he knew it was a flag to attract his attention, and sure enough, there was Becky, lying naked on the ground, in the middle of a patch of soft grass. Gabe pushed his horse right up to the girl, so that he could look straight down at her. "What do you think you're doing?" he demanded.

She had a very pouty look on her face. "You didn't think you were just going to ride away from me with a handshake, did you?" she demanded back.

She was lying with her legs slightly parted. Now he could see a gleam of wetness between those lovely thighs. "No . . . I guess not," he said, grinning for the first time since he'd seen the posse.

"Really?" Becky squealed in delight as he swung down off his horse. The pout was gone now, replaced by a look of eager, simmering anticipation. Events followed quite rapidly, as rapidly as Gabe could get out of his clothes. As he lay down on the grass, the girl was all over him, pressing her body close to his, smothering his face with her breasts, rubbing the wet heat between her legs against his side.

There was not much for him to do. As soon as Becky realized he had an erection, she straddled him. She began rubbing her crotch against him frantically. The tip of his penis caught at the edge of her vagina. "Oh!" Becky yelped. A second later, she was hammering her hips down, until she had engulfed him.

Gabe lay on his back, studying the girl above him, mesmerized by the intensity of the ecstasy mirrored on her face. He watched her first orgasm, saw her throw her head back, eyes staring into nothing, watched the muscles in her neck tense, saw the way her stomach muscles sucked inward.

For a few seconds after the orgasm Becky sat motionless above him, shuddering. Then he began to move inside her again. The girl's body responded with a slow undulating roll of her hips, that quickly grew into the beginning of another orgasm.

Orgasm followed orgasm, until the final screaming, writhing culmination that had Gabe coming with the girl, flooding into her. With one last shuddering gasp, she collapsed on top of him. "No more," she panted. "Please . . . no more. You'll kill me."

She lay on top of him for several minutes, while he gently stroked her sweat-slippery back. He felt her breathing slowly return to normal. Finally, she sat up, and grinned down at him. That almost-nineteen-year-old grin of triumph and elation, of new things discovered. "Are all men as good at this as you are?" she asked breathlessly.

"That's not the kind of thing I'd be likely to know, is it," he replied in amusement. "I suppose there's really only one way to find out."

She shook her head vehemently. "Uh-uh. You're the only one I want."

But he had seen the sudden gleam of interest, of speculation in her eyes, for just a brief second before she'd replied. A vista of imagined lovers. He felt a little pang of loss, of jealousy, but also, a sense of relief. No matter what happened between them, or didn't happen, Becky would come out of it all right. She might be in love with romance, with passion, with drama . . . but she was no fool. Gabe would be willing to bet what little he had that Becky was a natural survivor.

She made no protest as Gabe put on his clothes and remounted. She did not move toward her own clothes; they were scattered over quite an area. She stood on the flattened patch of grass, her face still flushed from their lovemaking, her breasts swollen, the triangle of hair between her legs matted and damp. "You come back and see me!" she said fiercely. "You hear?"

He nodded. "I hear. And I will."

And he meant it. He turned his horse and rode away, toward the trail. He'd only gone about forty yards when he stopped his horse and looked back at the girl. She stood, still naked, looking after him, a slender shaft of beauty in the midst of the wilderness. A sprite, a fairy, a spirit of the forest. A spirit of passion and sensuality. A young woman filled with a curious kind of lust-filled innocence.

It was an effort for Gabe to turn his horse and ride away.

CHAPTER ELEVEN

Gabe did not immediately ride all the way down to the plain. When he was several miles from the Jackson place, he branched off into a small valley. He could tell, from the greenery that lay ahead, that the valley had plenty of water. He would need water.

It took him another hour to find the place he wanted, a little meadow surrounded by a thick screen of trees and brush. A small stream flowed just to one side of the meadow. It was a perfect place for *initi*.

Gabe dismounted, unsaddled his mount, then staked out the big stallion right in the middle of a stretch of particularly rich grass. He then began to collect firewood, the driest wood he could find, so that there would not be much smoke. He used his knife to whittle a crude digging tool, then scooped out a shallow hole in which to build a fire. He laid wood in the pit, some of the pieces pointing north and south, others east and west. He then started the fire.

While the fire burned hotter and hotter, Gabe wandered down to the stream, looking for stones. They could not be just any stones; he had to avoid the kind that would explode when they grew hot, or that would crumble into dust. Over the next ten minutes he gathered ten such stones, each one three to five inches across.

Returning to the pit, he laid the stones on the fire, which was already showing a nice bed of coals. In a while, the stones would be hot enough.

He returned to the stream. Taking out his knife, he cut a dozen slender willow shoots and began to peel the bark from them. When he had them completely peeled, so that they gleamed white, and had cut them to the right length, he knelt and began to dig holes in the ground with his knife, a dozen holes, arranged in a rough circle about seven feet across. He stuck the butt end of each willow shoot into a hole, then tamped it in tightly. He bent the poles inward, then, using the stripped bark, lashed their ends together until he had fashioned the framework of a dome about four feet high. He stepped back. Good. It was beginning to look like a sweat lodge.

While he could still see what he was doing, he dug another shallow pit, right in the center of the dome. Then he went to where he had stacked his gear, looking for blankets and coats to cover the dome. He used his saddle blanket, sleeping blankets, some of his clothes, even the heavy buffalo hide coat that he usually carried rolled up behind his saddle. Eventually he was satisfied that no light, or very little light, would leak inside the sweat lodge.

Then he began to prepare himself. He was already half-naked, with his shirt and jacket draped over the sweat lodge. Now he stripped off the rest of his clothes, and walked down to the stream. Time to cleanse himself. He really should have done so the moment he arrived. Or, better yet, as soon as he'd left Becky. He was a hunted man, there was always the danger of a fight. And to fight after making love to a woman, without having washed himself, was to invite death. Just as it was dangerous to approach the spirits, to perform a ceremony, to ask for help, while he was unclean.

Gabe had been among the whites long enough to know the white man's view of what he was doing. Superstition. But he'd seen white men go into churches and do all kinds of strange things, while supplicating their gods. All he knew was that what he did made him feel right. Made him feel clean, strong, confident. As far as he'd

been able to discover, the white man had nothing better
to offer. What worked, worked.

Gabe quickly washed himself in the stream. Then he
returned to the fire, naked under the bright sun, happy to
feel the clean air drying his wet skin. The rocks looked
about ready, they were almost white-hot.

He pulled up some aromatic shrubs, the driest ones
he could find, and crawled into the lodge through the
single opening he had left, laying the shrubs near the
central pit. He went back for his canteen, and laid it
beside the shrubs. Then he cut a pair of forked sticks,
which he used as tongs, to transport the heated stones
into the lodge. He had to avert his face from the heat,
and when he got into the dim interior of the dome, he
could see that they were glowing white-hot.

Gabe worked until he had stacked all the stones into
the central pit. Then he went back to his gear. Reaching
into his saddlebags, he extracted a bundle wrapped in
deer hide. Unrolling the bundle he took out a pipe, along
with some smoking mixture.

Everything was ready now. Gabe scooped up a hot
coal with his wooden tongs, then carried the coal, along
with the pipe, into the lodge. He set the pipe down on
the ground, and dropped the coal into the pit, where it
glowed against the shimmering rocks.

It took him a few seconds to correctly close the flap
of cloth that was to cover the entrance. Then he crawled
across the floor of the lodge and sat, cross-legged, facing
the pit. Almost no light came inside, but the glow of the
rocks, plus the red, glowing eye of the coal, gave him
enough light so that he could see what he was doing.

Initi. The act of cleansing his *ni*, his . . . How would
the white man put it? His spirit? Better to think of it as
the force that flowed into him, through him, something
that he breathed in and out. The force that held together
all that existed, everything that lived and breathed, even
the rocks.

His *ni* had grown weak, confused, partly because of
his wound, but also because he had not been nurturing it,
he had not been paying his spirit the attention it merited.
Too much time had been spent making love to Becky,

too much time in a white man's house, cut off from the earth, his original mother.

But now he was ready. First, he would smoke. He picked up the pipe. How terrible it would have been if Josh, the bartender, had sold the pipe, or destroyed it. This particular pipe, along with a few other items, made up the center of Gabe's possessions, special belongings that had become a part of him.

The pipe itself had been given to him by an old Oglala warrior and medicine man named Two Face . . . minutes before he was hanged by the army. Two Face, wanting to make peace with the whites, had purchased a white woman who was being held captive by another group, with the intention of returning her to her own people. An act of peace. Of course, he'd raped her along the way, in all innocence, since that was what captive women were for. So, when he brought the woman in, the army had beaten him, then hanged him, but not before he'd surreptitiously dropped his pipe at Gabe's feet, in the cell they shared.

Gabe tamped his smoking mixture, *chanshasha*—a mixture of dried willow bark and tobacco—into the bowl of the pipe. He rubbed his fingers over the bowl; it felt smooth to the touch, reassuring. It was made of a special red stone, found in what the whites now called Minnesota, the original home of the Lakota, before they'd acquired horses and, using this marvelous new mobility, moved out onto the vast plains.

Using the wooden forks, Gabe picked up the single glowing coal and dropped it into the pipe bowl. The *chanshasha* began to smoke almost immediately. Holding the pipe bowl in his left hand, and the long hollow willow stem in his right, he gravely presented the smoking pipe first to the West, then to the North, the East, and the South, his mind full of the powers that dwelt there. Then he held the pipe down toward the earth, and finally, upward, toward the spirits of the sky.

Only then did he put the pipe to his lips and smoke, and as the pungent fumes entered his body, he could feel power flowing into him along with the smoke. The power of the spirits he had invoked.

He smoked until the bowl was empty. Then he put the pipe down next to him. Gathering a handful of the dried bushes he'd brought inside the sweat lodge, he threw them onto the glowing stones. In a few seconds the lodge was filled with aromatic smoke. He breathed it in, coughing a little.

Now . . . *initi* itself. He picked up his canteen and sprinkled water on a small switch he'd made of green leaves, then sprinkled water onto the hot rocks. With a loud hiss, steam began to rise. It had already been hot inside the lodge; and now, sitting this close to the white-hot stones, the steam pressed in on his skin, searing, making him gasp from the pain of it.

Gabe forced himself to sit still, tried to breathe normally. The steam rose around him, and he found that he could not catch his breath. Sweat was pouring from him. He felt claustrophobic, but remained where he was. To steady himself, he began to chant songs, special songs that had been taught to him by his Spirit Guide, the old Shaman, High Backbone. The man who had initiated him into the ways of the real world, the world that lies behind the one we think we see.

The steam was diminishing a little. Gabe sprinkled more water on the rocks. Again, that loud hiss as steam rose, this time accompanied by a sharp crack as one of the stones split under the impact of the cold water.

Over the next ten minutes Gabe sprinkled water on the stones twice more. And as the steam rose around him, as the sweat poured from his body, he opened his mind, his very skin, to the spirits with whom he wanted to communicate. It was not quite like prayer in the white man's way, not a simple asking for this or for that, it was more a merging of himself, his mind, with the power of the spirits, so that this same power would be available to him. Would be there to protect him during the dangerous times that lay ahead.

Finally, as the last of the steam died away, Gabe crawled from the lodge out into the open. The bright sun dazzled him for a moment, a perfect time for an enemy to attack, but he had known, inside the lodge, that there were no enemies near. Something had told him.

He ran down to the stream and threw himself into the water. Its coolness felt marvelous after the searing heat of the sweat lodge. He lay in the water for some time, letting the slowly moving current wash away the last of the dross that had been weighing him down. Leaving the water, Gabe stood for a moment on the grassy bank, looking around at the mountains, the grass, the stream, feeling the air flowing over his wet skin. It was there, all around him, Wakan-tanka, that which the white man called the Great Spirit.

A poor translation. To the Indian mind, Great Mystery might be better. No, that was not quite right, either. Great Mysteriousness. Something beyond the understanding of a mere human, but something indubitably out there, something of awesome power, that had formed, and still maintained, the entirety of existence. And if a man went about it correctly, he could feel Wakan-tanka all around him, be a part of it, participate in the very mysteriousness that he would never be able to understand with his mind.

As Gabe walked toward his saddlebags, he felt light, renewed, full of strength. He bent over the bags and pulled from them a small cutting of horsehair, died red. It had been a gift from his Spirit Guide, High Backbone, after Gabe's vision quest. The red color signified a connection to Wakinyan, the Winged One. What the whites called the Thunderbird.

Gabe sat on the grass, still naked, and began braiding the horsehair roach into his long hair, behind his ear. A sign that he was protected by Wakinyan himself. He had seen that in his vision, and as he slowly worked the roach into his hair, he thought back to the vision.

It had been right after he returned to the People, after escaping from the fort, from his jail cell. One of the first things he'd done was tell High Backbone that he wanted to undertake a vision quest. The old man had agreed that it was indeed time.

Four days Gabe sat on a hilltop, chanting, without food. And the vision had not come. It was only at the very end of his allotted four days that the vision had suddenly swept over him. A disturbing vision, which he had not immediately understood. Slowly, with the aid of High Backbone's interpretation, the confused images began to make sense. Uncomfortable sense, foretelling his separation from the People, the long road he would travel alone, among the whites. Foretelling the destruction of the People's way of life. And the death of his mother. He remembered that part of his vision with particular clarity, the golden strands of his mother's hair, lying at the bottom of a pit. A grave.

But the most powerful part of his vision had been the sudden appearance of Wakinyan himself, the sound of thunder as Wakinyan settled his mighty wings around Gabe's shoulders. As the great wings had enveloped him, Gabe had felt a sense of protection pour into his body. A sense of invulnerability.

At the time, he had not been called Gabe. He had a different name among the Oglala. When he'd been a boy of only fourteen, word had come of an approaching column of soldiers. Gabe had been the one chosen to carry the warning to a distant group of Oglala. For four days he'd ridden through a raging blizzard to deliver the warning, and as a result of his great accomplishment, he'd been given a new name, his manhood's name. Long Rider.

Memories. Of things long gone. When Gabe had finished braiding the horsehair roach into his hair he got up and quickly dressed. Then he thoroughly disassembled the sweat lodge, scattering its willow frame over a wide area. He did the same with the rocks. Then he saddled his horse and stowed his gear . . . all except for the big buffalo hide coat, which lay on the ground, back side up.

Gabe stood over the coat. Across its upper back was a brightly colored painting of Wakinyan, wings spread wide to envelope the shoulders of whoever wore the coat.

Gabe continued to look down at the painting, remembering. It was his mother's work. Right after his vision quest, she'd been cutting and stitching a new lodge cover out of cured buffalo hides. Proud that Wakinyan had appeared in her son's vision, she had decided to paint that part of it onto the lodge cover.

Then the soldiers had struck. Gabe had seen his new wife shot through the belly and head, and his mother run through with a saber. With a rescued Oglala baby under each arm, he'd been unable to intervene. Later, after the soldiers had burned the camp, then retired, Gabe had returned to find his mother's lodge destroyed . . . except for one section of the lodge cover. The part on which she'd painted the spreading wings of Wakinyan.

As he recovered from his grief, Gabe had sewed and stitched, until he had formed the remains of his mother's lodge cover into a heavy coat that reached almost to his heels.

He put the coat on now. It had been fashioned so that Wakinyan's spread wings arched across his shoulders, as they had in the vision. And as Gabe felt the painted wings settle across his shoulders, he had the same impression as he'd had during the vision itself. Of being protected, invincible, of strength and daring pouring into his body. This was his war coat.

Gabe checked his weapons. All were loaded and ready, for he was indeed going to war. Going to fight against corrupt and greedy men. And, as he swung up into the saddle, he stopped thinking of himself as Gabe Conrad, and became once again, at least until the fighting was over, Long Rider, Oglala warrior.

CHAPTER TWELVE

The three men were lounging around the fire, swapping yarns. Well, two of them were. From where he lay in the dark, about fifty feet away, Long Rider could see the differences in the men, in the way they acted. Two of them appeared to be just simple cowhands, but the third was a much harder-looking specimen. One of Cleary's gunmen. Or maybe Duval's. If there was a difference.

Long Rider had spotted the men the day before, after riding onto Duval's land. They were herding twenty head of horses. Long Rider had moved in close just before dark, and noticed that the horses wore a considerable mixture of brands. No doubt stolen. He figured the two cowhands were there to ride herd on the horses, and the gunman to ride herd on the cowhands.

Long Rider wriggled a little closer to the fire. The men were relaxed; the horses had been contained in a rope corral that boxed them into a little canyon. The two cowhands were the most at ease; the third man sat up straighter, constantly checking the night for sounds or movement. Long Rider knew he'd be the one he'd have to watch out for.

"Well, Luke," one of the cowhands was saying to the other cowhand, "guess I've had better jobs, but the pay's all right on this one."

Luke nodded a little doubtfully. "Never thought I'd end up bein' a horse thief. If my old man could see me now, he'd whup me till my skin peeled off."

The other cowhand fidgeted a bit. "Hell, Luke . . . we didn't steal 'em. We're just movin' 'em along. Nothin' wrong with that. I s'pose."

Luke shrugged. "Didn't have much choice, did we, Charlie? Duval said to take these here animals down toward Mexico, an' that's what we gotta do. Get on the wrong side o' Duval, and he'll feed you to Cleary."

Charlie nodded. "Yep. 'Course, if we was to leave the county . . . "

The gunman had been watching the two cowhands. "You try that, pilgrims, an' he'll just send me after you. Or maybe Cleary, or that new deputy of his, Rawls. Remember all that trouble you got into a year ago. You could hang for a thing like that."

"Well, hell, Jake," Charlie said angrily. "That trouble weren't rightly our fault. That dude an' his brother drew down on us. How was we s'posed to know them girls belonged to them? Didn't have no choice but to defend ourselves. Cleary don't have no call, holdin' ancient history over us, making' us work for Duval, stealin' horses—"

Luke cut in. "We didn't steal 'em, Charlie. Just herdin' 'em."

Jake snorted. "You two make me sick. Complainin' all the time, not doin' a thing about it."

He stood up. He was tall and thin. A long-barreled Colt .45 hung low at his right side. "You wanna complain," he snarled at the two cowhands, "you complain to me."

Luke and Charlie looked up at him warily. Jake remained standing over them, his right hand near the butt of his pistol. "Come on," he snarled. "I wanna hear your complaints."

"Oh, now, Jake," Charlie said lamely. "We don't want no trouble. We was just jawin'."

Luke was less cowed. "We're gettin' kinda tired of you pushin' us around, Jake." Luke was propped up on one elbow near the fire. He was wearing a pistol in an old floppy holster, hitched up high on his right side, but he made no move to get up.

Long Rider saw an evil grin split Jake's thin features. "Yeah?" he asked, almost gleefully. "Just how tired of me are you? You wanna stand up and do somethin' about it?"

For a moment Long Rider thought Luke was going to go ahead and stand up. He could see anger and fear warring against each other on the young man's features. Long Rider wondered if there really was going to be a shoot-out. If so, maybe Jake and Luke would kill one another. Then there'd only be one man left to deal with.

But more likely, Jake would kill Luke. And Long Rider had plans for Luke.

"Ah, shit, Jake," Luke finally muttered, staring sullenly down at the ground. "Some other day, some other place. We got horses to deliver."

Jake looked almost disappointed as his hand drifted away from the butt of his pistol. Now there's a man who likes killing, Long Rider thought. Likes it for its own sake. That kind of man should not be alive.

"Ah, you gutless nothings," Jake sneered. "It's a wonder those two brothers didn't kill you. You're the worst shots I ever seen."

"They was even worse," Charlie murmured. "Sure didn't like doin' that. Didn't like seein' 'em lyin' there, dead. Alive one minute, dead the next. They was real good-lookin' fellas. Young, too, maybe no more'n twenty, twenty-two. They was just worried about losin' them two women. Guess I woulda been, too."

"Women get men killed all the time," Luke said. Long Rider thought he could hear the sadness in his voice. He tried to tell himself that these two men were not cowards; they just did not like killing. But it was difficult for him to excuse them. He had felt contempt for the way they'd backed down in front of Jake. To him, raised an Oglala, there was nothing more contemptible than a coward. A coward was a man begging to be killed. How could a coward be left in his misery and shame? Besides, these two men had let themselves be forced into running stolen horses for a man they obviously disliked. Weak men. But probably not bad men. He decided he would let them live. If they let him do it.

Long Rider's original plan had been to simply steal the horses in the night. He'd grown up stealing horses. That was the favorite sport of the plains tribes . . . stealing horses and women. He remembered the times he'd crept up on a camp of sleeping Crow, or Pawnee, and stolen their mounts, almost right out from underneath them. Of course, sometimes he'd been on the other end of the action, with the Crow, or some other group, raiding Oglala stock and women. There'd been some hard fighting. Some losses and some gains. But what else was a warrior's life for?

The white man saw it differently. Instead of admiring stock raiders for their daring and skill, horse thieves were hanged. A miserable way to die; Long Rider hoped that when it was his time to die he got his in a quick hard fight. Remembering the old days, he itched to slip into that canyon during the small hours of the morning, when the alertness of the three hostlers would be at its lowest ebb, then ride away with three or four of the horses.

However, he wanted them all. That would hurt Duval and Cleary much more . . . to lose all twenty horses. And if he took all twenty, he would have to herd them. It would not be easy for one man to control twenty half-wild horses. And while he was trying, Jake and Luke and Charlie would undoubtedly be hot on his trail. Which meant that he would have to use a different plan. One that no one would expect of an Oglala-trained horse thief.

The little camp rose shortly after dawn. Luke awoke first, stretching himself, trying to work out the aches and stiffness that came with sleeping on hard ground. Not that he noticed it much anymore; he'd been sleeping on hard ground, or hard bunkhouse mattresses, since he'd been a kid.

Charlie woke up next, lying in his bedroll, blinking at Luke as he moved around the resurrected fire. "Damn," Charlie muttered, yawning. "That coffee you're makin' sure does smell good."

"Well, git yer ass outta your fart sack an' gimme a hand with the bacon," Luke replied good-naturedly.

Charlie slid out of his bedroll, then went to stand near a bush, in his long underwear, taking his morning pee. When he came back toward the fire, he was scratching his armpits lazily. " 'Nother day, 'nother dollar," he muttered, yawning.

Charlie was pulling on his pants when Jake woke up. Jake was a man who woke up completely, all at once. No yawning, no stretching. Just . . . awake. The first thing he did was slide his pistol out of his bedroll, laying it on the ground next to his clothing. Only then did he get up and begin to dress.

Luke was still in a good mood. Apparently he'd either forgotten, or chose to ignore, the unpleasantness of the night before. He gestured toward Jake's pistol. "Ya know, Jake, some night that there thing's gonna go off, when you make a mistake an' reach for it 'stead o' your cock. Gonna blow your balls all the way to California."

Jake fixed him with a baleful glare. He might wake up quickly, but he seldom woke in a pleasant mood. "Hurry up with that grub," he growled as he buckled on his gun belt.

It was Charlie, bent over the frying pan, working with the sizzling bacon, who saw the stranger first. "Jesus Christ!" he burst out, dropping the pan into the fire.

The other two men turned to follow his bulging eyes. What they saw made them feel definitely uneasy. A man was standing about fifteen yards away, observing them. He was a tall man, with long, sandy-colored hair, and cold gray eyes. He was wearing an old slouch hat, and a long coat that looked like it had been made out of buffalo hide. He was also wearing moccasins, but he was clearly not an Indian.

The three horse thieves could see a revolver protruding butt-forward, cavalry style, from the man's right hip. But what bothered them most was the Winchester rifle he was holding in his hands. The rifle was pointed straight at them.

It was Jake who reacted first. "Who the hell are you?" he snarled.

"A whole lot of bad news," Long Rider replied coldly. "I'm taking these horses. They're going back to their rightful owners."

"Over my dead body," Jake snarled. "Gun him down, boys!"

He'd failed to consider that neither Luke nor Charlie had strapped on their guns. Not that it would have mattered. Jake's right hand was just beginning to move toward his pistol when the rifle roared. Firing from the hip, Long Rider put a .44 caliber bullet right through the middle of Jake's chest. Jake staggered backward, a look of shock and amazement on his face. His foot caught on a rock near the edge of the fire, and he fell backward, dead before he hit the ground.

Charlie and Luke were still frozen in place . . . it had all happened so fast, with Jake's command to fight almost drowned out by the immediate roar of the rifle. Then Jake, killer Jake, staggering backward, his gun still in its holster.

And more ominous . . . the sound of the Winchester's action as the stranger jacked another round into the chamber. "Oh, Jesus," Charlie moaned. He knew he'd never stand a chance of making it to his gun. Not the way the stranger shot.

"Just stand easy," Long Rider said, his voice flat but commanding, "and you'll live."

"Uh . . . yessir," Charlie muttered.

"And pull that man away from the fire. His foot's burning. I can smell it from here."

Charlie and Luke both turned quickly. Jake's foot was definitely on fire. The smell was terrible. Seizing his body under the arms, they dragged him several yards away, toward the edge of the campsite. Neither of the two cowhands made a move to take hold of Jake's pistol, although it was still in its holster, very close to their hands. They weren't going to take any chances. Not the way that tall son of a bitch could handle a rifle.

Long Rider walked into the campsite, holding the Winchester negligently in his right hand, finger near the

trigger. He'd watched the two men as they'd dragged
Jake's body away, wondering if they'd try for his gun.
They hadn't. That was good. He didn't want to kill them.
He needed them. "Where were the horses stolen?" he
asked abruptly.

"Huh?" Charlie stammered.

Long Rider repeated the question. It was Luke who
answered. "Over in Johnson County. Leastway's, that's
how I heard it."

"And you didn't steal them."

"Uh-uh," Luke said quickly. He thought about the
possibility of getting hanged; if they caught you with
stolen horses, they stretched your neck. "Some of the
boys rode over there, did a little collecting. We didn't
have nothin' to do with it. It was Jake, I suppose. He
came back with the horses."

"And you weren't worried about the owners coming
after you?"

"Hell, Johnson County's quite a ways off. We didn't
have nothin' to do with stealin' those nags. And even if
we had, Cleary ain't gonna let no posse come over this
way, anyhow."

"No. He wouldn't."

Said without emotion. The stranger was beginning to
make Luke more nervous than if he'd started shooting
again. Just no emotion there at all, those expressionless
gray eyes staring back at a man, with no way to read
what was behind them. Like a damn Injun . . . except
this sure as hell wasn't no Injun. Not with those eyes,
and that light-colored hair. "What you gonna do with
us?" he finally asked, wondering if he really wanted to
know.

"Watch while you finish cooking breakfast," Long
Rider said calmly. "I'm hungry."

So the two horse herders boiled the coffee, fried the
bacon, and warmed up a can of beans, while Long Rider
sat a few yards away, apparently relaxed, but with the
barrel of his rifle pointed more or less in their direction. Luke and Charlie kept looking over at Jake's body.
His foot was still smoking a little, and by now the flies
had found him. By the time the food had been cooked,

they discovered that they had little appetite. The stranger, however, ate with gusto, still seated several yards away, still with his rifle more or less pointed at them. He'd made no move to collect their guns. Luke doubted they'd live five seconds if they tried to grab them.

Long Rider did collect their weapons once he'd eaten. He unloaded both pistols, and Jake's rifle, then told the men to tie them onto the packhorse. And to make sure there was no more ammunition hidden in the rest of the gear. "If I find any, I'll kill you both," he said, again in that flat, matter-of-fact voice. Both Luke and Charlie knew he meant it. Every word.

It took half an hour to break camp. When all the gear had been stowed, Long Rider faced the two nervous punchers. "As I said earlier . . . we're taking the horses back where they came from. You say that's Johnson County. I assume you know where that is. I don't, so you'll lead the way, pick the trail."

"Johnson County!" Luke burst out. "They see these nags, they'll string us up to the nearest tree!"

"No they won't," Long Rider replied. "We found them. Killed the men who stole them, and we're bringing them back. For a reward. The white man understands people who do noble deeds for money. They won't hang us."

Luke and Charlie were not totally convinced, but there was not much they could do about it. "Let me make one thing clear," Long Rider said coldly. "If you try to escape, try to turn on me . . . if you even try to lead me into an ambush of your friends, you will be the first to die. Even if they eventually kill me. Do I make myself absolutely clear?"

"Real clear, mister," Luke muttered. He and Charlie had better do what this nut said. At least for a while. It was a three-day trip to Johnson County. A lot could happen in three days. This bastard would have to sleep sometime. Maybe then . . .

It was not that Luke wanted to be a hero. But he was almost as scared of his boss, Lew Duval, as he was of the man who'd just gunned down Jake. If Duval caught them taking the horses north, instead of south, he'd think they were stealing them. If that happened, death wouldn't be as quick for Charlie and Luke as it had been for Jake.

The first day's ride was easy enough, pushing the horses along, with Luke and Charlie riding out to the sides, chousing any adventuresome animals back into the pack. It was not that difficult; horses are by nature herd animals. They just needed a little encouraging from time to time.

Long Rider rode drag, so that he could keep an eye on the two other men. Luke figured that was one of the few good things about this whole mess . . . that cold-eyed son of a bitch was eating plenty of dust.

That night, camp was made as usual. As they got ready to bed down, Luke and Charlie gave each other a knowing look. Either the bastard had to eventually fall asleep, or if he didn't, he'd be exhausted tomorrow. Either way . . .

They were unprepared when Long Rider mounted his horse and started to ride out of the camp. "Hey! Where you goin'?" Charlie blurted out. Could it be this easy? Was the stranger growing tired of the whole thing?

Long Rider pointed to the darkness that surrounded the low flicker of the camp fire. "I'll be out there," he said. "Somewhere. Keeping an eye on you."

They watched him disappear into the night. Wordlessly, both men crawled into their tattered bedrolls. But they did not find falling asleep easy. "Charlie?" Luke hissed softly. "You awake?"

"Yeah."

"Let's see if we can get the hell out of here. Leave Duval's nags, get our own, and just ride."

"I dunno. . . ."

"Shit. That loco bastard could decide to kill us any time. We oughta git while we can. He's probably asleep by now."

"Maybe you're right."

Both men slipped quietly out of their bedrolls and began to collect their gear. A few minutes later Charlie picked up his saddle and bedroll and lugged it toward his horse, which was tied up near a big rock.

Except that there was something wrong. Very wrong.

That rock hadn't been there when they bedded down. He was sure of it. "Gawd!" he burst out when the rock moved a little.

Long Rider stood up. Charlie could see the glint of a rifle barrel. "Going somewhere?" Long Rider asked softly. The tone of his voice sent chills up and down Charlie's spine.

"Guess not," Charlie muttered. He turned to walk past Luke, who was standing, frozen, his gear still clutched to his chest. "Come on," Charlie hissed to Luke. "Let's get these rolls spread out 'fore he decides we oughta go to sleep forever."

Charlie threw his bedroll down on the ground. He could not resist turning around, to see if the stranger had followed him. Damn! He was gone! Just disappeared into thin air. Maybe turned himself back into a rock.

Both cowhands quickly got into their bedrolls. Once again, both men had a lot of trouble getting to sleep. "Luke?" Charlie whispered.

"Huh?"

"I didn't hear a sound. Not a fuckin' sound. One minute he wasn't there, the next he was."

"Yeah. Spooky."

"Luke?"

"Yeah!" There was a little more irritation in Luke's voice this time.

"I think we better stop figuring on gettin' away. Don't you think so?"

A moment's silence. "Damned right. Now let's get some shut-eye. We got a long day ahead of us."

Having given up, they did sleep well, and were in fairly good shape all through the following day. Nothing more was said about trying to get away, or of overpowering their captor.

When they reached the Johnson County seat the afternoon of the third day, no one paid much attention to three man herding a band of twenty horses down the main street . . . until someone recognized a horse as one that had been stolen from him. "Thief! Horse thief!" he shouted, running after the herd.

By now they had reached the center of town. Long

Rider picked out what he figured was the sheriff's office. "Run the horses down to that big corral at the other end of the street," he told Luke and Charlie. "I'll be busy here."

People were congregating; more locals had recognized stolen stock. A big burly man came out of the sheriff's office. He had a badge pinned to the front of his shirt. Long Rider had heard from Luke and Charlie that the local sheriff was honest. "What's going on here?" the big man demanded.

"Recovered some stolen stock," Long Rider said curtly. "Had to kill the thieves to do it. My associates are taking them down to the corral now. I figure you can sort out what belongs to whom."

The sheriff looked up at him suspiciously. "And just how did you manage to run across the men who stole the horses?"

"I'm a bounty hunter," Long Rider lied. "My business is finding thieves. Killers. But there was no reward out on the men who did the stealing, so I figured maybe there'd be a reward for bringing the horses back."

The sheriff still looked suspicious. "Maybe. I'll have to ask the owners. What might your name be, mister?"

"Rider," Long Rider replied.

"Just Rider?"

"That'll have to do."

The sheriff considered for a moment. Out in these empty spaces, the local thinking was that a man had the right to choose how he'd be called. "Well, Mr. Rider. You just hang around the area for a day or two. We'll see what we can do about a reward. There was some mighty unhappy people around here . . . losing all that stock. Who the hell did it?"

Long Rider let a moment's silence pass. "Why don't you ask Sheriff Cleary, over in the next county. Or Lew Duval. They might have some answers for you."

The sheriff's face darkened. "So that's the way it is. Those mangy sonsa bitches. I . . . never mind."

Long Rider could have read the other man's frustration. Cleary had his domain sewn up. He was the local law. Obviously, Johnson County had had its troubles with

Cleary and Duval before . . . and had not been able to do a damned thing about it.

Luke and Charlie came riding back. Long Rider was glad they had not tried to run; that could have given away the whole thing. He looked hard at them. They looked nervously back. "Run, and you'll hang," he said in a low voice. "Shoot your mouths off and you'll hang just as high. Stick by me and you'll be all right. Do you understand?"

The two cowhands nodded obediently. They were amazed that they were not already in the county lockup. They followed Long Rider to the town's only hotel, where they took two rooms . . . Long Rider alone in one, the two punchers in another.

Long Rider knew they were not home free yet. The local sheriff might figure that it had been a setup. That they might have stolen the horses, then brought them back to collect a reward. A little thinking ought to convince him that it wasn't likely; they could have gotten much more from selling the horses down at the border than by settling for a simple reward.

They got the reward the next day, not a lot of money, but still enough to have made the ride worthwhile. Luke and Charlie were further amazed when Long Rider gave them each thirty dollars. "If I were you," he told them quietly, "I'd start riding and keep riding, until you reach someplace where the people have never heard of either Cleary or Duval."

The two punchers, overjoyed to be alive, and with a month's pay in their pockets, rode out immediately. Long Rider stayed in town for a while longer. He had a letter to write.

An hour later he came out of his room with the letter in his hand. He posted it at the town's tiny post office, then walked to his horse. He slipped the remaining money into his saddlebags. He had not taken it for himself, but to use against Cleary and Duval, when he got back to their county. Because he wasn't finished with them yet.

As he rode out of town, he reflected on the wording of his letter:

To John Cleary, or Lew Duval, although I doubt
it makes much difference which one of you gets
this first. The other one will see it soon enough. As
a gesture of thanks for the hospitality you showed
me while passing through your area, the free room
and board, and the healthy outdoor exercise, I felt
obliged to take the horses you had found, and return
them to their rightful owners. I told them where
the horses came from. Understandably, they are
appropriately grateful for your part in the operation.
                                          —Long Rider

Still, there'd been something missing, something he
would have liked to do.

He'd ridden several miles before he realized what it
was. He would love to be there, to see their faces when
they read the letter. A damned shame, but you can't have
everything. He rode on, smiling, imagining.

CHAPTER THIRTEEN

Long Rider considered heading for the Jackson place. He would like to see them again. Face it . . . he'd particularly like to see Becky. But in so doing, he might endanger all of them. No, not that, either—that was not why he was hesitating. If he returned, he might lose his edge, his fighting spirit. He might lose it somewhere on Becky's eager body. Or, more accurately, inside it. He felt very strong at the moment, very ready for more action. *Initi* had helped. So had the action itself, when he'd taken the horses.

What more could he do? He thought back to the letter he'd written Cleary and Duval. He'd thanked them for their hospitality, meaning the chain gang. He let himself think about the chain gang, the prison camp, and how he had hated what they'd done to him. He remembered the man he had met there. Charles. He also remembered how Charles had died, fighting, alongside him, to escape.

The chain gang. The more he thought about it, the more Long Rider's anger grew. He would do something about the chain gang.

It was a hot day. The prisoners were sweating as they moved dirt and broke up rocks. The guards were sweating, too. Hidden behind some brush, Long Rider watched as the guards patrolled back and forth, watching the convicts alertly. Apparently, the fate of Bull and the guard who'd died with him had considerably sharpened discipline.

That was good in a way, because the guards were watching the prisoners, not the land around them. If he could get close enough . . .

But the land was too open. The closest he could get was twenty-five yards. If he tried to rush the guards from that distance, they'd see him too soon, they'd turn those sawed-off shotguns on him, and he'd be shredded before he got halfway there.

He could always shoot them from ambush, but he didn't want to do that. Not because he didn't think the guards deserved killing—all of Cleary's guards seemed to be brutal—but because of the effect it would have on the prisoners. Many, faced with aiding a man who'd just killed two lawmen, would want nothing to do with him.

So it had to be by surprise. What he needed was for the guards to get close enough together so that he could take out both of them at the same time. But how? They were patrolling quite correctly, spaced out nicely.

The heat. That might be his ally. He watched one of the guards wince in pain as his hand touched the barrel of his shotgun, which had been heated by the relentless sun. He saw the patches of sweat ringing their shirts. He also saw the only shady place around . . . underneath a large cottonwood, about twenty yards away from the toiling line of men.

Gabe waited. Waited for lunchtime. When he'd been on the gang, the guards had let the prisoners rest for half an hour, less for their benefit than for the guards. At lunchtime the prisoners were all bunched together, instead of strung out, giving the guards a chance to sit down together and swap lies, while keeping an eye on their charges.

Gabe began to move slowly along the ground, crawling sometimes, running bent over when the cover was good enough. Half an hour before noon, he reached the single cottonwood, wriggling into the brush that rose thickly right behind it. He lay down to wait, conscious of how hot it was, feeling the soil all around him radiating heat.

Finally, noon. "All right, you jailbirds," Gabe heard one of the guards call out. "Get your asses together over here."

The men straggled over, exhausted from the heat and the backbreaking labor, dragging their tools along behind them. They came together in an untidy mass about twenty yards from the cottonwood tree. Gabe had expected that; the supplies were stacked there.

Gabe watched as one of the guards proceeded to chain all of the men together, while the other guard stood watch, shotgun ready. The first guard stepped back, his work done. Now the men would have to move all together or not at all. They were chained into one helpless mass.

One of the prisoners began to distribute the food, such as it was. Indigestible slop, Long Rider remembered, mostly starch, designed to barely keep a man strong enough to keep working. The guards picked up their own better supplies. Would they sit down and eat right next to the prisoners? If they did . . .

No. One of the guards was already looking over at the cottonwood. "Let's get us some shade," he said to his companion.

Long Rider watched them walk over toward the tree. This was the most dangerous time, when they were facing his hiding place. He lay absolutely motionless, even closing his eyes so that they would not give him away by reflecting light. He let out a soft breath when the two men reached the cottonwood, then sat down, facing away from him, toward the prisoners.

The two guards each pulled a sandwich from a metal lunch box. Beef sandwiches, as usual. Long Rider remembered those beef sandwiches. When he'd been a prisoner, he'd been able to smell the meat, the good bread, the pickles they often had with their lunches. While he and the other men starved.

He began to inch forward.

"Goddamn, it's hot!" one of the guards said to the other.

"Yeah. I'd like to have me one of them easy, indoor jobs. Maybe inside a nice cool adobe. Better yet, a bar, with lots of cold beer."

The first guard nodded. "Uh-huh. But I guess we're lucky to have any work at all, the way things go around here."

The second man nodded. "Yeah. This sure beats chasin' cows."

A shrug. "I suppose so. Kinda makes you think, though, the way Bull and Jack got killed."

"Yeah. They never did get the guy that did it, did they?"

"Long gone. 'Course, I guess Bull might have been askin' for it. He was one mean son of a bitch. If I was one of them prisoners, I'd o' took my first chance at him, too."

"Well, hell, it's the nature of the job. Maybe Bull had the right way. . . . "

The man suddenly started to turn as he sensed movement behind him. "Hey!" he shouted.

In a blur of speed, Long Rider burst from the bushes, six feet behind the two men. The one who'd seen him start his move, the one who'd shouted, turned just in time to catch the barrel of Long Rider's pistol across the top of his head.

He fell like a poleaxed steer. His companion, startled into immobility for a split second, recovered himself and started to bend down, to reach for his shotgun, but Long Rider thrust the muzzle of the pistol into the man's face, then cranked the hammer back. "Uh-uh," he said, shaking his head warningly.

The guard heard the hammer going back. He looked up, to find himself staring down a .44 caliber hole that looked the size of a railway tunnel. He slowly backed away from his shotgun. His eyes flicked from the gun muzzle to the man holding it. "You!" he said, his eyes widening in recognition. He'd been a guard when Long Rider had been a prisoner.

"I'm glad you know who I am," Long Rider said coldly. "So you know that if you don't do exactly as I say, I'll blow your head off."

The guard nodded jerkily, still staring down the muzzle of Long Rider's pistol. Long Rider noticed that both men had extra arm and leg chains dangling from their belts. "Chain him up," he told the guard, pointing down at the unconscious man.

The guard did as he was told, although Long Rider could see that he'd recovered his wits somewhat. He was clearly trying to figure out some way he could turn the tables.

He never got the chance. Long Rider spun him around, then slipped chains over his wrists. Next, he looped a longer chain around the bole of the cottonwood, fastening each end to the chains binding the arms of the two guards, so that they were chained to the tree.

Now he turned his attention to the prisoners. They had seen it all, of course, and were watching him fixedly. Long Rider tore the key chains away from the guards' belts, then tossed them to the prisoners. "Those of you who want to leave, unchain yourselves," he said.

Not all of the prisoners chose to escape. "I only got three more days to go," one man said. "I don't wanna be no fugitive."

Four men chose to run. Long Rider had to force them to stay away from the guards; they wanted to beat the two men to death. Long Rider chained the other six men to the cottonwood tree, next to the guards, in case the guards convinced them to run for help. He took the keys with him. It would be hours before anyone found them, so he left the water and food within easy reach.

The day was wearing on. He'd spotted another work crew earlier, and he headed for it now. This time it was easier; one of the guards had stepped into the brush to take a leak. When he didn't come back, the other guard went to investigate . . . and got a rifle barrel across his skull.

Half a dozen more prisoners decided to make a run for it. That pleased Long Rider; the sheriff would send men after them. Men who would not be available to come after him.

Long Rider hid the guards and prisoners in thick brush. Now he went out to the work site. Good. He'd heard

the sound of blasting earlier, and sure enough, stored
far away from the prisoners, he found half a dozen
sticks of the new explosive, giant powder. Dynamite,
some people called it. He took all six sticks, then faded
into the brush, found his horse, and rode away, toward
the distant mountains. He made sure the guards saw
him heading that way. But once out of sight, on hard
ground that would show few tracks, he angled off to the
side. Within half an hour he was riding back almost
the way he had come . . . toward the work camp where
the prisoners were locked up each night.

He was in place about an hour before dark. Hidden
in thick brush, he watched as the camp burst into activ-
ity. Apparently the chained guards had been found. A
horseman went racing toward town. Just before dark he
returned with a dozen more horsemen. A posse. Long
Rider saw Rawls among them. Just as dark was falling,
the prisoners who had chosen not to escape were brought
back. Long Rider watched as they were herded into the
shacks where they slept.

He was too far away to hear much of what was being
said, but just after dark the posse rode away, accompanied by the four guards Long Rider had captured.
Apparently the guards were riding along to help identify
any escaped men they might find.

Long Rider continued to lie in the brush, watching
night routine take over the camp. As far as he could see,
there were only two guards left; the rest had ridden off
with the posse. One was in the watchtower, the other
patrolled the buildings. Just two men, alone. However,
they must feel secure; the prisoners were all chained to
their bunks. And there were fewer of them than normal.

When he judged that the two guards had had enough
time to fall into a mind-numbing routine, Long Rider
slipped through the brush, heading for the camp, taking his Winchester and a bag containing the dynamite.
The moon obligingly set just before he reached the wire
encircling the camp. It was extremely dark.

He was aided by the camp design. The tower, which
overlooked the whole camp, had been placed right next
to the wire. It was held up by four stout supports. Long

Rider carefully placed a stick of dynamite against the two supports closest to the fence. Trailing fuse behind him, he then crawled to the big gate, and placed the rest of the dynamite.

He crawled back about ten yards, holding the ends of both sections of fuse. He waited for the guard patrolling the buildings to disappear behind one of them. He'd already noticed that the guard in the tower spent most of his time looking into the camp, rather than out of it. He hoped he was too bored to change his routine.

Long Rider lit the fuses, then, when they were both sputtering, stood up and sprinted for cover, rolling into a shallow ditch about fifty yards from the camp.

He heard a startled cry. One of the guards must have spotted the burning fuses. Too late. The man's cry was drowned out by a thunderous roar. Long Rider hugged the ground hard. A few seconds later, debris began to rain down around him. When no more seemed to be falling, he seized his rifle, got up, and ran toward the camp.

The tower, with two of its support legs blown off, had toppled over onto its side. Its descent had been slowed when it hit the wire, but the wire had broken, and the top of the tower, where the guard was, had hit the dirt hard, outside the wire. It had been partially shattered by the explosion, and further demolished when it struck the ground. Long Rider raced up to the guard, who lay motionless, obviously unconscious. He picked up the man's shotgun, and threw it far into the dark.

The gate was a shambles. Long Rider ran past its wreckage, looking for the other guard. He was standing next to one of the buildings, scorched and stunned. He'd dropped his shotgun; Long Rider scooped it up and threw it inside one of the buildings. A moment later the butt of his rifle connected with the man's skull, knocking him unconscious.

There was a lot of yelling coming from the sleeping quarters. Long Rider ran to the office, which had been partially wrecked by the explosion. Large key rings hung on nails. He snatched them all, then walked back to the sleeping quarters. "You men!" he shouted. "Unlock your chains and get outside. All of you."

When no one seemed to move inside one of the shacks, he fired his rifle into the ceiling. "I said outside!" he roared.

Within less than ten minutes, all of the prisoners were outside. "You again?" one of them asked. He'd been among those who'd declined escape earlier in the day.

"Yes. Me."

Long Rider quickly canvassed the prisoners. The most bitter among them, the most eager to strike back at the corrupt system that had put them here, he ordered to collect combustibles. Kerosene was splashed inside all the buildings. The cook shack was left for last. He watched the men loot the best of the food, and drag it out into the open.

Then Long Rider fired the entire camp. Within half an hour after the dynamite had exploded, every building was blazing, including the ones holding all the tools and stores. Cleary's chain gang profits were going to be badly chewed up.

There were horses in the stables. Some of the prisoners mounted them and rode away. As earlier, others chose not to leave. When Long Rider left, about twenty men were standing in an awed group, watching their prison burn, while they ate all the food they could choke down.

After reaching his horse, Long Rider mounted. He didn't ride away immediately, but watched the burning camp. It lit up the sky. The posse would notice the flames soon, and ride back to investigate. They'd know who'd done it, plenty of prisoners would mention the tall man wearing the long buffalo hide coat, with the Thunderbird painted on the back. They'd know. Cleary and Duval would know. Particularly after the letter. They'd be after him. They'd be raging mad, wanting blood. His blood.

Well . . . let them try and take it.

CHAPTER FOURTEEN

By morning, Long Rider was many miles away, riding across a flat, somewhat loamy plain. Stopping his tired horse, he turned in the saddle and took a good look at the long line of tracks that stretched away behind him. A one-eyed tracker with mail-order glasses could follow them easily. Good.

Long Rider kept riding. He turned to the right, so that his route now paralleled a low, flat butte, which was several hundred yards to his left. It wasn't a very high butte, but the edge of it was steep and crumbly. No way to get either man or horse up that cliff.

The butte was also quite long. At its western edge a trail led upward, between it and another butte. Long Rider knew the trail well; he'd been over it previously.

The trail wound on for miles. Finally he saw the opening he'd seen before, a barely noticeable track leading past some bushes. He stopped to study his back trail again. For the past several miles he'd been doing his best to avoid leaving any marks of his passage. He knew that a good enough tracker would eventually be able to pick up his trail, maybe find a stone his horse's hoof had kicked aside, or a broken twig that had caught a tuft of horsehair. He wondered if this area had a tracker that good. At least, a white tracker. He doubted the Cleary bunch would give an Indian the time of day.

Long Rider carefully nosed his horse past the bushes. Then he dismounted. Taking part of a dried branch that had broken off a large shrub, he went back and methodically obliterated any marks that might have indicated where he turned off the main trail. Finally, satisfied, he remounted, and urged his horse up the trail.

The trail was steep and slippery. Sometimes he had to dismount and lead his horse. After half an hour's hard work, he finally reached the end of the trail. The butte's flat, featureless top stretched away ahead of him. He rode across it quickly now, he'd have to hurry; he doubted he had more than a couple of hours' lead over anyone who might be after him, and he'd used up a lot of that lead detouring around the butte.

Finally he was in position. He staked his horse in a small depression that had been hollowed out by wind and rain. Taking his Sharps, his bedroll, his binoculars, and two boxes of cartridges, he quickly moved to the edge of the butte, where he crouched, hidden behind a bush, then looked over the edge.

The plain stretched away below him. He adjusted his binoculars and studied the ground outward from the butte. Yes, there they were down below, the clear hoof marks of his horse, leading in from the plain toward the butte, then turning off toward the west. He moved the binoculars higher, scanning the horizon. At first he saw nothing, but as he continued to scan, he believed he saw movement about a mile away.

He lay the glasses down, then went back for his bedroll, which he placed near the edge of the butte, at the edge of a little stone lip. Lying on his stomach, he slid the forestock of the Sharps onto the bedroll. It fit solidly. He made sure that the rifle's barrel was camouflaged as much as possible by some small bushes.

He picked up the glasses again. Yes, definite movement, now coming closer. Slowly, the movement resolved into a dozen horsemen, riding along at a slow trot. He saw a man in front looking down at the ground.

Undoubtedly at the tracks Long Rider had left so clearly imprinted in the soft soil.

The posse. Amazing. Was a dozen men all they'd been able to get together? Well, they'd been losing a lot of men lately. Long Rider was pleased. From this vantage point on the bluff, high above them, he thought he could handle a dozen. Twenty would have been stretching it.

He flipped open the breech of the Sharps, then rummaged in a box for one of the huge cartridges. He slid it into the chamber, then closed the breech.

Nothing to do now but wait. The horsemen rode closer and closer. He let them get to within five hundred yards. They chose to stop at that point. The leaders seemed to be arguing. A flash of light from the chest of one of the men indicated that at least one deputy was with them.

The distance was great, but it was a clear, quiet day, with absolutely no wind. From his high perch, Gabe could just make out some of the words, especially when one man raised his voice. "I tell you, Forbes, I don't like it. These tracks are too damned clear."

Another man, Gabe thought it was the deputy, shouted back, "What the hell do you want, Jason? Tracks we can't follow? Hell, stumbling onto this trail is a break, and you know it."

"I don't know any such thing," Jason snapped. "This is one smart dude; we all know that. He wouldn't of left tracks like this for us to follow. It's got to be a trap."

Gabe picked up the binoculars. He saw the deputy scratch his head. "Well . . . "

Then the deputy's voice rose again, and now the tone was one of disgust. "Hell! Maybe we just picked up the tracks of one of those idiot prisoners. Maybe we've wasted a whole damned night."

"No," Jason insisted. "It's him. Remember the bend in his horse's shoe? We picked that up at the place where he coldcocked those guards."

"So, then," Forbes insisted. "We're in luck. Let's stop jawin' and git after the bastard."

Long Rider laid down his binoculars and picked up the Sharps, fitting the butt of the big rifle snugly against his shoulder. He carefully cocked the hammer, using the trigger to make sure it didn't make too much noise. He already had the leaf sight raised, with the sliding crossbar set at five hundred yards. He sighted in on a target below, then settled himself, slowing his breathing, relaxing over the rifle, with his finger slowly applying pressure to the trigger.

Kablam! The Sharps's heavy report thundered out. The butt slammed back against Long Rider's shoulder, jolting his relaxed body. The bullet flew true. Forbes was just about to set his horse into motion when the massive slug, all seven hundred grains of soft lead, slammed into the animal's side. "What the hell . . . ?" Forbes burst out, just a second before the distant sound of the shot finally reached them.

By then his horse was already falling, killed instantly. Forbes barely had time to kick free of the stirrups. The posse members were frozen in place for a second or two, during which they heard the distant *clunk-click* of a big buffalo gun being cocked. "Scatter!" one man shouted.

But it was too late. Another horse went down, screaming and kicking. This time, the horse wasn't killed instantly. Its rider kicked himself free, then, cursing, put a bullet through the wounded animal's head.

Another distant report, another animal down. Now the posse did scatter, but they really had nowhere to go. The plain was too flat. Only scrawny bushes spotted its emptiness, hardly substantial enough cover to stop a heavy caliber bullet.

By now they had spotted where the shots were coming from; a thin fog of white gunsmoke hung above one spot at the very top of the nearby butte. "There he is!" the deputy shouted. "Git him, boys!"

Rifles crashed. But most of the posse members were armed with lever-action Winchesters, which fired what in reality were pistol cartridges. Their range did not even extend as far as the top of the butte. The deputy cursed as he saw bullets strike the base of the bluff.

Kablam! Another horse went down. By now the posse members were trying to keep out of danger by zigzagging their mounts. The horses would, of course, wear out. Retreat would be the only option. Charging the butte, over all that open ground, under such accurate fire, was a good way to get killed.

However, not all of the men were armed with .44-40 or .38-40 Winchesters. One of the men had the new Centennial model, caliber .45-75. It did not throw as big a bullet as the Sharps—350 grains against the Sharps's 700—but it was a damned sight better than the lower caliber weapons. "Jimson . . . get that cannon of yours up here," Forbes shouted.

The man with the Centennial, grinning now that he was going to get to show off his new rifle, which all the others had been ribbing him about, flopped down behind a horse and opened fire at the smoke up on the butte's rim.

Lead began to fly uncomfortably close to Long Rider. The Centennial was a lever-action model, and could fire much more quickly than his Sharps. On the other hand, he was a lot harder to see up here on the butte's rim.

Long Rider abandoned the horses and concentrated on the man with the long-range rifle. He had not wanted to shoot any of the men. A full-scale slaughter of lawmen could cause a reaction that would ruin his plans.

But the man with the rifle was going to have to be dealt with. Long Rider sighted carefully, fired. The bullet hit the horse right in front of the rifleman. Blood and tissue sprayed over his face, blinding him for a moment. He spluttered in indignation, and rose up a little, to wipe his face.

By then, Long Rider had fired again. It was a lucky shot; the bullet hit the Winchester, ruining the action, then bounced off, its energy partly spent, to slam into the man's shoulder. It was not a very good hit, but it rammed him backward. He wouldn't die, but he wouldn't be firing his rifle again, either. No one would.

Long Rider killed another horse. He did not particularly like killing horses, he did not particularly like killing anything, but he had a Lakota's pragmatic view of animals. If it was a danger, kill it. And since mounted men were a danger to him, what better approach than to kill their mounts.

By now the posse had had enough. "Let's get the hell out of here, boys!" Forbes shouted. " 'Afore we ain't got nothin' left to ride."

Long Rider put another couple of bullets close while the men loaded their wounded rifleman on a horse. Then they pulled back, almost half of them riding double. After they had ridden back about a hundred yards, Long Rider stood up. They saw him silhouetted against the sky, a tall figure wearing a long, dark coat. They stopped, looking back up at him, sensing he would not fire again.

His voice floated down to them. "You men," they heard him call out. "You're riding for an evil man. John Cleary. I'll tell you now . . . riding for Cleary will get you killed. Dead."

He let that sink in, then added, "And for what? So he can get richer and richer off your blood? Enough men have died. Abandon Cleary. Let control of this county go back to the people who live here. Cleary's finished. So is Duval. And any of you who ride for either one will be finished just as certainly."

He turned, then, to walk away from the edge of the butte, and as he turned, those with good eyes could see that he had some kind of figure painted across the back of his coat. One man had binoculars. He passed them around. Those who looked could see that it was an image of what the Indians called the Thunderbird.

Then man, coat, and image were gone, disappearing behind the butte's protective heights.

CHAPTER FIFTEEN

As he rode down the back side of the butte, Long Rider found himself wondering what to do next. He'd certainly exacted a large measure of revenge for what Cleary and company had done to him. Some of Cleary's men were dead. That gun hand of Duval's, too. Their operations were in a shambles. . . . Had he done enough by now? Was it time to stop?

He was strongly tempted to simply ride away. Ride out of this county, this country, and head off in the direction he'd been heading when he'd had the bad luck to drink the doped root beer in Josh's saloon. Wanderlust was as much a part of Long Rider as his arms and legs. He'd grown up among a nomadic people who, except in winter, when moving was difficult, had usually packed up their lodges every few days and moved on, following the buffalo. For Long Rider, the far horizon had always been enormously tempting.

Yet, something was holding him here. Becky? The fact that Cleary and Duval were still riding high? He realized that he did not quite know.

So he headed up into the mountains again, searching, looking for the right kind of place. He found it late in the day, a high, remote valley, rich in water, wood, and game. He rode into the little valley as the sun was approaching the western horizon. He sat his horse at the valley's edge, looking down over the vast sweep of mountains and plain below him. He watched the shadows lengthen, felt the air soften, sensed the total isolation that surrounded him, and he thought, this is a good place for deciding.

His first night's camp was simple—just a bedroll near a small stream, with his horse staked out on a long lead rope. He lay on his back, watching the first of the stars come out. The world fell still around him. At first there was just the soft chuckle of the stream, a light breeze rustling the treetops. Then, bit by bit, the first stirrings of the night creatures began. The soft swoop of an owl, followed by the shrill, thin cry of the mouse it had caught. Distantly, a coyote howled. He heard the sound of thumping in the bushes not far away. A rabbit. The night terror was beginning for rabbits and other small furry creatures, as claw and fang began the evening hunt.

Gabe awoke as the first pearly gray light appeared in the east. He lay on his back, in no hurry at all. Hands locked behind his head, he watched the sky continue to brighten. At last, the great fiery ball of the sun appeared above a nearby mountain peak.

He got up. Taking off his clothes, he washed in the stream. The water was invigoratingly cold. The day grew warm quite quickly. He abandoned his white man's clothing, digging a breechclout out of his saddlebags. Then, dressed only in the breechclout and his moccasins, he began to explore the valley.

It was less than a mile long, and perhaps a quarter of a mile wide. It appeared that no one had been here for a very long time. There were no signs at all of mankind, no ruins, no destruction. Perhaps no human had ever set foot here. There were nothing but game trails, and short green grass, and wood and water. And the animals. He was going to have to start thinking about the animals. His food supply was very low.

He would not need food today. He set about building a sweat lodge, and when it was done, Long Rider performed *initi* again, this time in no rush at all, since he had no place to go, nothing special he wanted to do.

He built himself a small lean-to shelter, in which he sat, smoking his pipe. He let the day wear on, without time, without thought, without goal. Only late in the afternoon did he busy himself, setting snares on small game trails.

He was about a hundred yards from his camp, pegging down a string loop, when he became aware of movement about thirty yards away. He looked up. A big buck was standing just within a fringe of trees, alertly watching him. It was a fine animal, with many-pointed antlers rising high above its head.

Long Rider thought about his rifle, which was back in the lean-to. But he did not want the sound of gunfire to disturb this quiet little valley; there were undoubtedly many men hunting him. Nor would he be able to use so much meat; he knew he would not be staying here for long. "Go," he said softly to the buck. "It is not yet our time to meet."

The buck's head jerked up at the words. With a graceful leap it vanished back into the trees. For several seconds Long Rider heard it crashing through the brush. Then . . . the silence of the valley descended once again.

When he awoke the next morning, he walked his line of snares. Two rabbits had been caught. They hung in the tightened loops, strangled. Or perhaps their racing hearts had simply burst from fright, as sometimes happens with rabbits.

On the way back to his lean-to with the two rabbits, Long Rider passed through an area where several quail had nested. Small caches of eggs lay half-hidden beneath bushes. He helped himself to one egg from each nest, leaving the others to hatch—unless Coyote, the trickster, discovered them. Or a badger. Or rats, or lynxes, or any of the other creatures that kept the numbers of quail from reaching too high a level.

Back at the lean-to he skinned and cleaned the rabbits, and impaled them on long sticks, which he suspended between uprights over a small fire. And while the rabbits slowly cooked, he roasted the quail eggs next to the hot coals. He had eaten the eggs long before he judged the rabbits were ready.

Then, another day of sitting, and of thinking-by-not-thinking. And, by the third day, he had decided. He did not know enough. His information about Cleary and Duval was incomplete. He had taken care of all that he did know about: the horses Duval had stolen, and the shame of the chain gang. Now he must find out in what other areas Cleary and Duval were vulnerable. Because he knew that he had not yet finished with them, no matter how strongly the far horizon might call.

He left the valley on the morning of the fourth day, but before leaving, he carefully removed all traces of his having been there. He took apart his lean-to, and the sweat lodge, and scattered the various parts into the brush. He even smoothed the ground. His horse had trampled a lot of grass, but it would grow back quickly enough.

He was careful, riding back down the mountain. He stopped often, scanning the trail ahead with his binoculars. He saw no one during the entire journey. He reached the Jackson place late in the afternoon. He sat his horse in a stand of pine, studying the yard. Hal was outside, doing something to one of the small outbuildings. A thin stream of smoke was rising from the kitchen stove pipe. Mary must be cooking dinner. Long Rider began to realize how hungry he was, how ready for a big, hearty, meaty meal.

And then he saw Becky walk out the front door. She had a bucket in one hand. She stepped down off the porch and walked around to the side. A small stream ran behind the house. She must be on her way to fetch a bucket of water for Mary.

The stream ran between the house and Long Rider. He headed his horse toward the streambed, riding out of the bushes just as Becky was straightening up with a full pail of water. She must have sensed movement; she looked up quickly. "Oh!" she exclaimed when she saw Long Rider sitting his horse about fifteen yards away.

The sun was full on him; she could not have mistaken him for someone else. Yet she made no move in his direction. He realized that she was looking at him in a way he'd never seen her look at him before. There was something in her eyes, some new emotion. He tried to identify it. Fear? Awe?

And then her face broke into its usual bright, precocious expression, and laughing, she ran toward him. She stopped, though, when he made no move to get down off his horse. They studied one another for a few seconds. "You look, well, kind of . . . different," the girl said hesitantly.

Long Rider looked at her somberly. Then he smiled. "And you look wonderful."

He quickly dismounted. She came into his arms with a little rush and a whimper. "You scared me," she said. "You looked so . . . so dangerous. And I guess you are. We heard what you've been doing. You sure hit 'em hard."

Together, they walked back toward the house. "Boy," the girl said. "That's some coat. Makes you look real . . . scary."

Long Rider realized he should have taken off the Thunderbird coat before approaching the house. But over the past few days he had felt good wearing it. Perhaps it was time for Becky to see him as he really was.

Hal saw them enter the yard, with Long Rider walking beside Becky, leading his horse. Hal stiffened for a moment, then he let out a whoop and came walking toward them. "Heard you've been acting like a one-man army," he said, grinning.

His grin faded a little as he neared Long Rider. Then he said it, too. "You're different."

Long Rider shook his head. "Not really. You just didn't look hard enough before."

Mary had heard the commotion. She came out onto the sagging porch. Long Rider saw that she was studying him intently. He also noticed that her face did not alter its expression. If she saw a change in him, she welcomed it. It was all there for him, her warm, smiling welcome, and almost instantly Gabe stopped being Long Rider.

Half an hour later, they were all gathered around the table, making inroads on the big roast Mary had cooked.

"You got thin," Mary said accusingly. "You look like a starved cat. Eat up."

He ate up. The meat was delicious. And as he ate, they questioned him, first a little hesitantly, then with insatiable curiosity. "You only killed one man," Mary finally said. "Duval's horse thief. And those chain gang guards . . . you let them live, even though they're scum. And when the posse came after you, you only killed their horses."

"Right."

She looked perplexed. "But . . . why? When you could have wiped out so many of them?"

Gabe hid a smile. Mary was beginning to remind him more and more of a Lakota woman. It was the women who were harshest with the tribe's enemies. Pity the enemy who fell into their hands. Pity the man who had threatened their village, their children. He wondered if Mary might be pregnant, if an instinctive desire to protect her family was operating within her. Maybe not. Maybe she was just a very angry woman.

"I had no desire to harm the other two horse thieves," he explained. "They were simple working men who'd made a mistake. They were not fighters at all. As for the others, the men in the posse, the guards, I thought it would be best not to harm them. Even if they were working for corrupt men, they were the law. If a lot of them had died, more law would have been called in."

"But," Mary said in exasperation, "you killed Buck, and those two guards when you escaped from the chain gang."

Gabe's face grew bleak. "That was different. That was a fight. It was me or them. I just made sure that it turned out to be them."

A little silence fell over the table. "I think it was a good move," Hal finally said. "Everybody's heard about what Gabe did, about returning the stolen horses, the way he tore up the county work camp, how he stopped Cleary's posse. And I'll tell you something that's starting to happen. They're starting to laugh. Laugh at Cleary. Ordinary people, who, up until now, have figured Cleary and Duval are unstoppable. That anybody who goes up against them is going to get hurt bad. Now they see that it isn't necessarily true. That's why it's important it wasn't a bloodbath. A lot of killing would have scared them, instead of making them laugh. And laughter might bring down Cleary quicker than anything else."

Gabe nodded. He hadn't completely thought of it that way, but his instincts had guided him. He had played it the white man's way.

Hal seemed to grow a little uncomfortable. "They're talking a lot about you in town. About that coat you wear. About the name you use. Seems that quite a few people have heard of someone called Long Rider."

"Is that really you?" Becky asked excitedly.

"That was my name among the People."

"They say you're an outlaw," she added, almost hopefully.

He glanced around the table. They were all looking at him uncertainly. "I'll let you answer that question for yourselves," he finally said.

Hal shook his head. "It's already answered. If you're an outlaw, then so am I. Because I'm against the law, in the form of our crooked sheriff. We won't have any more talk of outlaws around this table."

The mood lightened. After dinner, they all went outside, to sit on the porch, so that they could watch the sun go down. The talk became general. Gabe gently led it back to Cleary and Duval, looking for other openings, other ways to go after them.

The subject of deeds came up. Hal began to talk bitterly about the loss of his ranch. "You know," he said, "I still got a deed to the place, registered over in the next county. But there's another deed sitting right down there in Cleary's county offices. A tax lien that says Duval bought the place for back taxes. Taxes that I never owed. That deed of theirs makes my deed worthless."

Gabe started to nod. He'd heard parts of this story before. Then something Hal had said jolted his consciousness. "Wait," he interrupted. "You said something about having a deed over in the next county. Why would it be over there?"

Hal shrugged. "Used to all be one huge county. Johnson County, the place where you took back those stolen horses. Then, a few years back, Johnson County got split into two parts. Just too much land for a single county government, a single sheriff. But I had my land before the split, and the deeds were registered in Johnson County. The original deed is still there. It's registered in the county book. But that damned tax deed of Duval's makes my deed worthless."

Gabe nodded slowly. "Are there more cases like that? Where Cleary and Duval have taken people's land, but the deeds are in two counties?"

"Sure. A lot. Half of what Cleary and Duval own. And they both have a lot of land they got by stealing from other people."

A small smile tugged at Gabe's lips. "And the only claim they have of ownership, the only papers that nullify the Johnson County deeds, are in town. Am I right? In Cleary's offices."

"Sure. In the Country Clerk's office. They . . . "

Then it began to dawn on Hal. "Wait," he said, holding up a hand warningly. "You're talking about something really dangerous. That office is right in the middle of town. Surrounded by Cleary and his deputies. You'd never . . . "

Gabe shook his head. "Not me. Us."

He looked straight at Hal. "Are you willing to take a chance?" he asked quietly. "To get your land back?"

"Well . . . of course. But . . . "

Gabe nodded. No need to say anything more. Not yet. Not until it was time to start planning his next move. Because he now knew how to strike back at Cleary and Duval in a way that would hurt them far more than anything he'd done so far.

CHAPTER SIXTEEN

Gabe could see that Hal was excited. His face was flushed, and his eyes glittered strangely. "You sure you want to do this?" Gabe asked, for about the fifth time.

The excited glitter in Hal's eyes changed to faint annoyance. "I've been waiting a long time to do something against Cleary. Now let's get on with it."

Gabe nodded. Hal would do. "Okay. Then let's mount up."

Hal nodded, then swung up onto a big black horse. He only had two horses, and this was his favorite. It was a stallion, like Gabe's, and just as mean.

Gabe covertly watched Hal, to see how he handled the animal. You could tell a lot about a man by the way he managed a horse. Hal swung himself right up into the saddle, no hesitation. The stallion snorted, and began to fidget. Hal called out a low-voiced but stern command. The horse's eyes rolled a little, but Gabe noted that the stallion immediately calmed down.

Gabe mounted his own horse. It was a little bigger than Hal's horse, but not by much. They were both handsome animals. Gabe wondered if the other stallion could keep up with his own . . . if they were pushed by bad luck to ride hard. He hoped so.

They had led both animals a hundred yards from the

house. Behind them, Mary and Becky were sweeping the yard with jury-rigged twig brooms, erasing any signs of that distinctive shoe that had helped the posse follow Gabe's horse. Gabe halted a moment, to watch Becky work. She was bending low, which caused the seat of her jeans to stretch in a most interesting manner.

He felt a glow of heat inside his body. If anything, the girl's sexual appetite seemed to have increased while he was away. Or maybe it was her idea of him in his new guise—new to her—as a warrior. The buffalo hide coat seemed to excite her enormously. She'd insisted they make love lying on it. He remembered how she'd moaned and whimpered and cried out, her strong young arms and legs locked around him, drawing him down into her body.

Enough. It was foolish to think of women and sex before going into a fight. He pulled his horse around, and rode out of the yard. Hal followed behind, having a little difficulty with the stallion at first, but within five minutes he'd reestablished in the animal's mind just who was boss.

They rode wide of the trail, over ground covered in pine needles. Gabe wanted no tracks to show where they had passed. Hal rode up alongside him. "I still think it's risky, doing what you plan on. They're real likely to catch you. You'll be right in town. . . . "

"And they'll be out of town."

Hal shrugged. "Sure hope so."

They rode for three hours, until they were several miles from town. Gabe began studying the ground carefully. "This is about right," he finally said.

"Yeah."

They were on a little ridge. The main road to town lay just below them. Gabe had Hal ride the black down to the trail. "Get him to stamp around a little," he called out. Hal did just that, milling the horse in a wide circle. Then he turned and trotted him back in a wide circle, until he had once again reached the ridge. He rode up to Gabe. "Guess it's time. Right?"

"Should be. They'll be along in an hour . . . if your information is right."

Hal nodded vigorously. "I'm sure it is. One of the deputies was drunk the other night, bragging about what a great operation they've got. Mary heard him."

"Okay . . . on your way."

"Be careful," Hal said. He touched his hat, then turned the big stallion and rode away, back toward the mountains, but in a different direction than the one they'd used to get here. Gabe sat his own horse, watching Hal grow smaller in the distance.

Time to get things rolling. Gabe got down from the horse and unrolled his Thunderbird coat, which had been tied in a bundle behind the saddle. He slipped it on, feeling as he did so the weight of the leather, feeling also the same sense of power, the power of Wakinyan, flooding through him. Cleary and his bunch were going to see a little more of Long Rider, whether they wanted to or not. In the meantime, there was nothing much to do but stay hidden and watch the trail.

The two men were careless. It was a carelessness born of never having had any trouble on this particular run. The dangerous part had been taking those damned horses down to the border, to sell them. It hadn't only been the danger of getting caught as horse thieves, but also that those thieving Mexicans would have stolen the horses themselves if they'd had a chance. But it had gone well enough. The rest of the boys were still down at the border, drinking tequila and screwing Mexican whores. God, those women down there were something else! Get 'em started and they never wanted to stop. Both men would have given half their wages to be there now, a brown-skinned girl on each arm. Which was about what it would have cost them anyhow.

But somebody had to bring the money back. A small sack of gold lay in the saddlebags of each man. As usual, the money would go straight to the ranch, Duval's place, after they checked in with Cleary. Both men admired Duval; that son of a bitch had his fingers in more pies than they could even imagine. Of course, they knew plenty of the money would end up in Cleary's pocket. Now *there* was a man who knew how to run a county.

One of the men smiled. Nothing like working under a sheriff who knew how to steal. And better, who knew how to get away with it.

With town only a few miles away, both men perked up a little. There were whores in town, too, and whiskey, and a hot bath to wash off the trail dust, and a big steak dinner at the hotel. So interested were they both in what lay at the end of the trail that neither was paying much attention to the terrain on either side.

They did not see the man ride out of the brush to their left. "Up with your hands," the man called out sharply.

Two heads swiveled. A rider was sitting a horse uncomfortably close, about thirty yards away, leveling a rifle at them. "What the—?" one of the horse thieves snarled. He started to reach for his own rifle; the butt was sticking up close to his hand.

The stranger fired, shattering the rifle stock. Splinters of wood stung the horse thief's hand. He thought of going for his pistol, but at thirty yards, pistol against rifle was just another form of suicide. The stranger had already levered another round into the chamber, and appeared to be aiming straight at his chest. "Hands *up*, I said," the stranger repeated, his voice like a whip crack.

Two pair of hands went into the air. The stranger had them carefully, very carefully, toss down their weapons. Then they were told to dismount. The stranger did not dismount until after they did, getting down on the far side of his horse. Even if they got to their weapons, he'd have had the advantage of the cover of his horse's body.

It did not take the stranger long to find the two bags of gold. They watched in impotent rage as he slipped the gold into his own saddlebags. Then he mounted. Looking down at them, he said, "Tell Cleary and Duval that I'll put this money to better use than they would have. I'll use it to fight them."

He turned his horse and rode away, trotting quickly up toward a ridge. The last they saw of him was the painted Thunderbird design disappearing over the ridge.

The two men mounted. "Oh, God," one of them said. "Duval's gonna kill us for losin' that gold."

"If Cleary don't first." He hesitated. "Think we oughta go on into town? Or just ride on outta the county?"

The other man shook his head vehemently. "Then they'll think we stole it. And they'll send somebody after us. Like that weird son of a bitch, Rawls. Naw . . . we gotta go back and tell 'em we were hit."

The two men rode briskly toward town. To make it look better they lashed their horses into a mad run a mile outside town. By the time they pulled up in front of the sheriff's office, their horses were convincingly lathered.

To their amazement, Cleary did not question their account of being robbed. Especially after they told him what the robber looked like; the big Indian bird painted on the back of his coat, the cold gray eyes, his marksmanship. Both men had been out of the area for nearly three weeks. They knew nothing of the man who'd been terrorizing Cleary and Duval.

Cleary did. "That son of a bitch has gotta be caught!" the sheriff roared. Rawls was in the office. "Get a posse together," Cleary snapped. "Right now. We ride in half an hour."

However, it did not prove easy to gather as big a posse as Cleary had hoped for. Few men answered the call, and most of those who did were not men Cleary would have preferred. He asked Rawls about it. "What's the matter?" he snapped to his deputy. "Why didn't you round up more men?"

Rawls shrugged. "When they heard it was this Long Rider character, a lot of 'em chickened out. Somebody was shootin' his mouth off at the saloon the other night. Told a lotta tall tales about that hombre, how he never misses, how he can sneak into a camp at night and cut everybody's throat while they're asleep."

"Oh yeah?" Cleary snarled. "Where is this yahoo with the big mouth?"

Rawls smiled. As with most of his smiles, it was not pleasant to see. "I run him out of town. After he spent a couple of days in the hoosegow for drunk and disorderly. The fine cost him a real nice gold ring."

Cleary paid no attention. "Well, we'll ride with the men we got. Should be enough to take care of one man."

"Hell," Rawls murmured softly. "I'm enough to take care of that Indian-lovin' bastard. All by myself."

"Then how come you ain't caught him?" Cleary snapped. Rawls's head came up, and there was a dangerous glint in his eyes, but Cleary was already striding out of the office.

The posse rode out ten minutes later, eight men, some of them characters Cleary wouldn't normally let sweep out the jail. He always paid his posse members, knowing that money could breed a kind of loyalty. The usual price for riding with a posse was twenty dollars a head, taken out of county funds. Thirty a head if they caught whoever they were chasing. Looking at this ragtag posse, Cleary considered halving the amount this time. Halving it? Hell, these yahoos weren't worth a dollar apiece. But then the word would get around that he'd dropped the price, and it would be even harder to recruit new posse members. *Damn* that bastard in the Indian coat.

They rode straight to the place where the robbery had taken place. The two horse thieves were with them, despite their protest of being tired from their long ride. They pointed out the spot. Cleary looked up at the ridge Long Rider had disappeared behind. "Let's get after him, boys," he shouted, and led the way toward the ridge.

The ground was sandy up to the ridge, but they could see the smudged prints of a single set of horse hoofs, both coming down toward the trail and heading back up toward the ridge.

Once on the other side of the ridge, the tracks took off straight toward the distant mountains. They rode along after them. The ground grew firmer, without being too hard to take a print. It was Rawls who said, "Yep . . . that's him. Same little bend in that right front shoe."

They rode hard after the tracks. Two hours later they were near the mountains, and still the tracks ran straight. A high ridge lay ahead. The tracks ran up close to it, then turned off at a right angle, paralleling the ridge. They all knew the area well enough to know that ten miles farther along a trail led up onto the heights above them.

Alarm bells went off in Cleary's head. "Whoa, boys!" he called out. "He's trying the same trick again . . .

wants to bushwhack us. Watch out for that ridge."

"Couldn't be," one of the men insisted. "He wouldn't have had enough time to get up there yet."

But Cleary insisted they ride well clear of the ridge, out of range of even a big Sharps buffalo gun. "Look!" Cleary shouted. "I was right! He was up there waitin' for us to get close enough."

Sure enough, a figure came to its feet up on top of the ridge. The figure of a tall man wearing a long dark coat, and carrying a rifle in his right hand. The distant figure looked down at them for a few seconds, then turned and moved away out of sight. Cleary whipped a pair of binoculars to his eyes. He had a single glimpse of the broad-winged Thunderbird painted across the back of the man's coat. "It's him, all right! Let's get up on that ridge!"

They rode hard toward the distant trail that would take them up onto the ridge. But one posse member was not satisfied. He rode up alongside Cleary. "I don't like it," he shouted over the steady sound of the hooves. "There ain't no way he coulda got up there that fast. It's another one of his tricks."

"Maybe he knows another trail," Cleary snapped back. "Keep your eyes peeled for where he turned off. We're gonna get that bastard."

But no other trails showed themselves. However, once up on the ridge, at the point where they'd seen Long Rider disappear, the tracks of his horse led off up into the mountains. They were easy to follow, and follow them the posse did, urged on by Cleary.

Many miles ahead of them, a tall figure on a black horse and wearing a long coat slowed as he approached a stream. He studied the ground ahead of him. The soil this side of the stream was soft enough to take tracks well. It was the same on the far side of the stream for about twenty yards. Then a streak of granite rose out of the ground, stretching away for several hundred yards. Beyond that there was only shale and scree.

The rider brought his horse right up to the stream. The animal stopped at the stream bank and lowered its head. The rider let it drink for a little while, then pulled

its head up. Then he urged the horse into the water. But
instead of crossing the stream, he rode upstream for a
while, until he found a patch of granite that came right
down to the water. He left the stream at this point, riding
out onto the granite. The horse's hooves slipped a little,
but eventually he had the horse where he wanted him,
just across the water from where his tracks entered it.

Now, the tricky part. Carefully, the rider began backing his horse toward the water. The animal reared its
neck a little, but it had been called on to perform this
maneuver before, and obeyed well enough.

Finally the horse was standing in the stream again. The
rider studied the tracks he had left. It sure as hell looked
like someone had ridden right on through the stream and
up onto the granite, where the tracks disappeared.

Satisfied, the rider, Hal Jackson, headed his horse
downstream, until several hundred yards later he reached
a patch of granite that permitted him to leave the water
again. Nothing to do now but ride on home. Very early in
the morning, Gabe had ridden his horse past that first
granite outcropping, leaving tracks that led way up into
the hills, where they petered out on hard ground.

Hal took a circuitous route home. When Mary and
Becky heard the sound of his horse, they came running
out of the house to meet him. "How did it go?" Mary
asked anxiously.

"I'm alive, ain't I?" he replied, grinning. "Come on
. . . let's get to work."

They led the horse into an outbuilding, where Hal
quickly removed the bent shoe they'd taken from Gabe's
horse, and replaced it with another. Meanwhile, the
women were once again going carefully over the yard,
erasing every sign of that bent shoe they could find.

Hal came out of the shed and tossed the horseshoe far
into the brush. Mary came up to him. "You should have
buried it."

"No. They probably won't even come here."

Hal led the way into the house. He took off his long
coat. It was Gabe's linen duster. Becky and Mary had
spent a couple of hours painting a copy of the Thunderbird across the back. There was a fire going in the stove.

Hal stuffed the coat inside. The smell of burning cloth and paint filled the air.

They were both silent while the coat burned. Finally, Mary spoke. "I wonder how Gabe's doing?"

Hal shrugged, but his face was worried. "I don't know. But he's sure stuck his neck out this time."

CHAPTER SEVENTEEN

When the posse rode out after him, Long Rider was not very far away. He had hidden himself on a little hilltop that overlooked the town. Studying the scene below through his binoculars, he saw the trouble Cleary was having getting together a posse. Finally, he saw what looked like most of the able-bodied, or maybe just willing, men ride out of town with the sheriff.

Long Rider remained on the hilltop for a while, engaged in silent debate. It would be a hell of a lot safer to wait until dark, then steal into town. But it would lack drama, and, after talking to Hal, he realized that open drama might bring down Cleary more quickly than stealth.

He waited two hours, long enough for Cleary and the posse to get well away from town. Then he mounted his horse and headed straight toward the town. He rode directly in, right down the middle of the main street, passing in front of the saloon where, at least for him, the whole mess had started. He was in full regalia, wearing the Wakinyan coat, the big painted wings clearly visible on the back, and with High Backbone's red horsehair roach braided into his hair. He looked straight ahead, as if he did not have a care in the world. He passed a couple of startled citizens, who stared after him in amazement.

He rode to the livery stable. Without dismounting, he rapped on the office door with the butt of his rifle. The liveryman came outside to see who was annoying his noon siesta. His mouth gaped when he saw who it was. "What? What the hell . . . ?"

"I want to rent a good packhorse."

The request was not delivered in a threatening tone, but the liveryman never considered refusing. Like everyone else in town, he'd been hearing tales about the man in the long buffalo hide coat. Within five minutes he had a pack saddle lashed onto the back of a sturdy animal. "Ah, how long are you gonna want him?" the liveryman asked hesitantly.

"Just for the day."

Long Rider flipped the man a five-dollar gold piece. The man handed him the lead reins, and Long Rider started away toward the main street, with the packhorse trailing along behind. He stopped about ten yards away from the liveryman and called back over his shoulder, "The sheriff will be bringing him back to you. Make sure he doesn't try to steal him. He does things like that."

Long Rider rode back down the main street, toward the county building. He dismounted and hitched both horses, his big black and the packhorse, right in front. He was just about to step up onto the boardwalk when he heard a voice call out from down the street. "You! Hey, you . . . Indian lover! You stop right there!"

He looked to his right. Rawls, the deputy who had come to the Jackson place, the one who'd insulted Becky, was striding rapidly along the street, straight toward him. Bad luck. Cleary had left a man behind.

Long Rider hesitated a moment, then decided he'd be better off down on the ground. Better footing. So he stepped off the boardwalk into the street, where he stood, waiting.

Rawls kept walking toward him. To Long Rider's surprise Rawls did not have a gun in his hand. But there was a revolver riding low in a holster on his right hip. Rawls stopped a dozen feet away, with his thumbs hitched in his gun belt.

A slow smile broke over Rawls's face. "I was beginnin' to worry we'd never meet," he drawled. The smile was slowly becoming a leer. "Not face-to-face. I was scared I'd get there too late, that somebody else'd get to you first, and all I'd find was your dead body."

Long Rider said nothing, just stood facing Rawls, apparently relaxed. But his eyes never left the other man's face.

Long Rider's direct stare began to bother Rawls. He tried to meet it, but it was like looking into open space. Cold space. He was searching for fear in the other man. He usually inspired fear in others, in the men he was about to kill. They were afraid because they knew they were going to die. But this hombre was different. There was nothing there at all. No emotion evident whatsoever. "You got a tongue?" Rawls demanded loudly.

Long Rider continued to stand facing him. Silently. Rawls's thumbs slid away from his gun belt. His hands were now hanging at his sides, the right hand close to the butt of his pistol. Still, Long Rider made no move. "I hear you're pretty good with a rifle," Rawls snarled. His gaze flicked to where Long Rider had tied his horse. Both rifles were still in their saddle scabbards. "But it's gonna be pistols now," Rawls continued. "And I never found a man who could beat me with a pistol."

He'd already noticed the pistol, resting butt-forward, on Long Rider's right hip. He'd also noticed Long Rider's twisted right trigger finger. Lefty, Rawls thought. He'll draw left-handed. The right don't work.

Curiously his opponent, despite Rawls's threats, still had his left hand nowhere near the butt of his pistol. His hand was idly toying with a button on the front of his shirt. As if he didn't care if Rawls drew his own pistol and killed him.

The first twinges of doubt began to affect Rawls. A little voice was nagging in his mind, *What does this man know that I don't?*

For the first time in his life, Rawls discovered himself fearing another man. Before, killing had been exhilarating, just plain fun, the excitement of seeing the other man begin to shake with fear when he realized Rawls was going to kill him. The actual pleasure of firing bullets into another man's body, watching the shock and pain on his face as the bullets entered, and then the terrible amazement as the man realized he was actually being killed.

Now Rawls was feeling some of that fear. And it was the fear that killed him. He tensed before he drew, something he usually never did, and it was this tensing that warned Long Rider that the other man was going for his gun.

Rawls still thought he was going to make it. Long Rider's left hand was nowhere near the butt of his pistol, so Rawls began to consider that he was going to draw with his right. Instead, Long Rider's left hand left the button it had been toying with, disappeared beneath the buffalo coat, and came back out holding a pistol.

All these observations were made in the split second that Rawls was reaching for his pistol. Time seemed to have slowed enormously, with everything happening in slow motion. Rawls saw the other man's pistol appear, and point straight at him. God, he was fast! Rawls was still bringing up his pistol, his thumb on the hammer, ready to cock it.

Rawls saw Long Rider's right hand hover over the hammer of his pistol. Saw the left trigger finger whiten as it pulled back the trigger, and held it there. Then the right hand was moving, open, fanning the hammer, and flame burst from the muzzle of the gun pointing at Rawls, a seemingly solid sheet of flame, as the shots thundered so close together that it was impossible to tell them apart.

Giant hammer blows slammed against Rawls's chest. He felt himself being driven backward. He was vaguely aware that he'd fired his own pistol, but he knew he had fired it at the ground.

Suddenly, everything was blue. It took Rawls a moment to realize that he was lying on his back, looking up at the sky. He sensed a shadow fall over him. He looked to the side. Long Rider was standing above him, his smoking pistol in his left hand. Rawls wanted to raise his own pistol and shoot the bastard, but there seemed to be nothing in his right hand. He raised the hand, looked

at it, then noticed the blood pumping out of his chest.
God! He was shot full of holes!

He tried to say something, some curse, because he
knew he was dying. But no words came, just blood,
bubbling up from his throat. And then shock, and pain,
and fear washed over Rawls, as he had seen it wash over
other men. And when he finally died, there was that same
look of sheer, disbelieving amazement on his face.

Long Rider looked down at the dead deputy for another
moment. He noticed that one of his bullets had punched a
hole in the tin star that adorned the other man's shirtfront.
Then Long Rider stepped up onto the boardwalk again
and headed for the county building.

It was just a two-room affair. When Long Rider
walked in the front door he was punching empties out of
his revolver and pushing home fresh rounds. Of course,
the county clerk had seen the whole thing, had watched
Rawls go down under Long Rider's bullets. The county
clerk was no hero, he knew who this man was, and what
he'd been doing. He sat at his desk, quaking with fear,
unable to move, sure he was about to be killed.

Instead, Long Rider looked at him with no evident
hostility. "Where would I find the deeds, and the deeds
registry?" he asked calmly.

The clerk discovered that his tongue was not working.
He pointed a shaking finger at a big wooden file cabinet.
"Good," the apparition in the long coat said. The clerk
watched as Long Rider slid the reloaded revolver back
into its holster beneath his coat. The clerk remembered
how quickly it had come out of that holster, and wondered if it would come out again.

"I want every deed that carries the name Cleary, or
Duval," Long Rider said. "Stack them up on that table
over there."

The clerk finally found his tongue. "But . . . "

Long Rider took a step toward him. "I want it done
very quickly. If it takes too long . . . "

The clerk jerked himself to his feet. Walking stiff-
kneed to the file cabinet, he opened the top drawer,
and began taking out papers. Long Rider moved a little
closer to him. "I'd be very disappointed if I discovered

later that you were unable to find all the right deeds," Long Rider said quietly.

Which was exactly what the clerk had been intending to do. He owed his job to Cleary and Duval. He knew this madman was going to do something bad to those deeds, but if he could save a few, there should be a lot of gratitude coming his way from his benefactors.

Long Rider's quiet words had a stronger effect than if he'd shouted. The clerk's pudgy little body jerked as if he'd been hit with a whip. He had visions of this man coming after him, probably in the middle of the night, stealing into his house, cutting his throat. Or maybe shooting him in the face. The clerk, like most men, had a horror of being shot in the face.

He pulled out the deed to every piece of property owned by either Cleary or Duval. When he had them stacked on the table, Long Rider spoke again. "And now . . . take the pages out of the ledger that records these deeds, and stack them with the deeds."

The clerk was dismayed. He'd hoped this mad killer would not have known about the ledger. But he did, and defeated now, the clerk mechanically put the registry pages with the deeds. He did not even resist when Long Rider told him to carry all the papers outside and shove them into his pack saddle. To do this, the clerk had to step uncomfortably close to Rawls's body. He noticed that flies were already buzzing around the corpse. He saw one fly crawl into the deputy's open mouth. Two more were crawling across his staring, sightless eyeballs. The clerk was sure he was going to be sick.

Finally, it was done. With the pack saddle stuffed with deeds and registry pages, Long Rider mounted his horse and rode off down the main street. The clerk sighed with relief as he saw him disappear around a corner. Now that the mad killer was leaving, the clerk suddenly found himself full of courage. He ran to the saloon and barged in through the doors. There were half a dozen men inside, hunched over their drinks. "The county records have been stolen!" he shouted. "We gotta get up a posse and get after that man!"

"Yeah?" one man said. "And are you gonna lead that

posse, Terwilleger? Or are you gonna leave it up to Rawls?"

The clerk knew, then, that no one was going to do anything. The sheriff, the man they all feared, was out of town, supposedly on the trail of the very man who'd just plundered the county records. And Rawls, the killer who'd been left behind to guard the town, lay dead in the street, covered with flies.

These men were scared. Or maybe not scared at all. Maybe that was it . . . they were losing their fear of Cleary, the man who'd dominated them for the past four years. They'd watched a single man make a fool of Cleary, gun down the killers he sent after him.

The clerk backed out the door. When he was in the street, he cast a quick glance at Rawls's body. Funny, he'd been scared to death of Rawls, and now he was nothing but dead meat. Maybe that was going to be Cleary's fate, too. Maybe it was time that he, John Terwilleger, County Clerk, stopped being afraid of that puffed-up bully.

When Sheriff John Cleary rode down out of the mountains, he could see the column of smoke from two miles away. A man had finally ridden out of town to tell him what had taken place in the county offices the day before. The man, a drunk who wanted to curry favor, had not found the posse until late in the morning. They had been camped at the point where they had lost the trail of the man they'd been following. Lost it for good. And now there was news that the son of a bitch had been tearing the town apart while they were off on a wild-goose chase.

When Cleary reached the source of the smoke he found nothing but smoldering coals and bits of charred paper . . . all that was left of the deeds and the pertinent pages of the registry. Whoever had set the fire—and Cleary had no doubt who it was—had been thoughtful enough to use the greasiest wood, wood that would smoke, so that Cleary would have no trouble discovering the extent of the disaster. Most of what he had worked for over the past four years had gone up in smoke.

Cleary looked around the area. A packhorse was tied to a tree not far away. The pack saddle looked like it had come from the livery stable. Cleary automatically thought about the probable value of the horse and pack, but desisted when the men around him stirred uneasily. Cleary growled out an order to one of them. "Ride out to Duval's place. Tell him I need him in town, just as fast as he can get there."

The man said nothing at first. Cleary looked at him angrily. Had he seen just a moment's hesitation in the man's eyes? "What the hell are you waiting for?" he snarled. He was reassured when he saw fear blossom in the man's eyes. A moment later Cleary was looking at the ass end of the man's horse as he pelted away. Good. He'd show the gutless bastards who still ran this county. What that Conrad bastard had left of it. "And one of you," he added, quite bitterly, "take that damned packhorse back to the livery stable."

When he reached town, Cleary was disturbed by the emptiness of the place. There was no one on the street. He saw a window shade flicker as a citizen pulled back from the window through which he'd been watching Cleary and the posse.

Cleary went straight to his office while someone else took care of his horse. Once inside, the first thing he did was open a cabinet and take out a bottle of whiskey. He poured himself a glass, and sat at his desk, sipping. Nothing to do now but wait for Duval to show up.

Duval reached town just before dark. He'd obviously ridden hard; he was dusty and tired-looking, and the horse that Cleary could see outside, hitched to the rail, was badly lathered. Duval always had been hard on horses.

Duval was a thin man of medium height, with a mean, pinched face. He dressed well, wearing a vest, string tie, and a dark coat. Duval's sartorial affectations had always amused Cleary. No matter how well he dressed, he still looked like a cheap chiseler. Which was just what he was. Still, Cleary had to admit that Duval had a damned shrewd mind. It was his ideas that had gained both of them so much power.

Duval sat opposite Cleary, studying his partner. He always worried a little about Cleary; he wasn't the brightest man who'd ever been born, but he sure could act. Duval noticed a nearly empty bottle of whiskey on Cleary's desk, and a half-full glass. Cleary's eyes were bloodshot. He looked nervous. Duval felt a little tickle of alarm. Was his strong right arm going to come apart on him?

"The man you sent out told me a little," Duval said without preamble. "You tell me the rest."

Baldly, flatly, Cleary filled Duval in on the latest disasters: Rawls's death, the theft and destruction of the deeds to their property. "You know what that means?" Cleary said bitterly. "Most of that stuff was already registered in Johnson County. If the former owners want to push their claims, they can just take back the land."

"If they've got the guts," Duval said bleakly. "They know what would happen to them if they tried."

"Oh?" Cleary asked bitterly. "Do they? What the hell can we do about it? Hell, I can hardly raise a posse anymore, and my best deputies have been killed. Shot down by that mad-dog bastard, Conrad. We shoulda killed that son of a bitch the moment we laid eyes on him."

"There should be something you can do about him," Duval insisted. "Hell, he's been running around killing lawmen, robbing people, burning records. Can't you call in help from outside?"

Cleary smiled bitterly. "You mean, like go to the Governor? Call in the troops, or the U.S. Marshal's office? Good thinking, Duval. Once outsiders get in here, they're gonna start nosing around. They're gonna find out what we've been doing. Do you want that?"

For the first time, Duval looked uncomfortable. "No . . . you're right. Can't have anybody poking around. But hell, Cleary, you're still the sheriff. Get together some more deputies. Hire them from outside, if you have to. We can still crack the whip around here. We've got the money, and we've got the power."

"Do we?" Cleary asked. "I've got some more wonderful news for you. Terwilleger, the county clerk, told me about it just an hour ago. You know that my term

as sheriff is up. The election is in a couple of weeks.
We didn't expect anyone to have the guts to run against
me. And now Terwilleger tells me that Hal Jackson rode
in here early this morning and filed. He's running for
sheriff, Duval. Running against me."

"Goddamn!" Duval burst out. "Does the man want to
commit suicide? He knows what'll happen to him if—"

"Does he?" Cleary interrupted with a bitter smile.
"Terwilleger said he rode in here with a dozen men.
Every one of them armed to the teeth. Each one of those
men has plenty of reason to hate me, Duval. Hate you,
too. And what have we got to fight them with? Dead
deputies and scared drunks."

Cleary stopped talking and took a close look at his
partner. When things got tough, he was accustomed to
looking toward Duval for a way out. And as he studied
Duval now, he was impressed. Duval was not panick-
ing. He'd known he wouldn't. Duval sat hunched in his
chair, his chin resting in his cupped right hand. Finally
he looked up. "Looks pretty clear to me," he finally said.
"It's this Conrad bastard, the one who calls himself Long
Rider, or something like that. He's what put iron in their
jellyfish backbones. He's gotta go. He's gotta be killed,
and they have to see him killed. Once they get a good
look at his dead body, you just watch. They'll back down
faster than a whipped dog."

"Great," Cleary snorted. "Isn't that just what we've
been trying to do for weeks? Kill the bastard? Haven't
had much luck, have we?"

Duval finally smiled. It was a pinched, ugly smile.
"The problem, Sheriff," he said sarcastically, "is that
you've been trying to do it all legally. With local tal-
ent. The office must be going to your head. What I pro-
pose is that we open up our purse strings and bring in
the best men money can buy. Manhunters. Professionals.
Then we'll see how well this long-haired son of a bitch
makes out."

Cleary didn't quite smile, but he nodded. "Yeah. Maybe it'll work. Real professionals. Real manhunters. And
after Conrad is gone, we'll start on Jackson. He'll maybe have a fatal accident, just before the election . . .

too late for them to put up another man. I like the idea, Duval. It might work. Hell, it *has* to work."

Duval leaned back in his seat. His wore a pleased expression. Like a cat who has just caught a mouse. "We'll even make it all nice and legal," he said. "You can deputize the men I bring in."

Cleary snorted bitterly. "Fine. God knows, I'm running pretty damned short of deputies."

CHAPTER EIGHTEEN

Long Rider had been feeling uneasy for the past two days. Perhaps it was the valley. Perhaps he shouldn't have returned to the same place. Or perhaps it was Hal, his candidacy for sheriff. Although Cleary and Duval seemed broken, Hal had made a very dangerous move.

Long Rider had been back in his little valley for four days. He'd encountered a smaller buck deer this time, and had risked the sound of a shot. The deer's meat now hung from drying racks he'd erected near his lean-to. He'd also discovered a berry patch about a quarter of a mile away. Perhaps, when the meat had dried, he would pound it to a powder, mix it with tallow and berries, and make pemmican. Not that he needed the pemmican; he could always ride to Hal's place and load up with supplies. But sometimes, using the old ways, the ways of the People, made him almost feel he was back with them.

After burning Cleary and Duval's deeds, Long Rider had ridden to the Jackson place. The news of his success had been met with great jubilation. Becky's eyes had shone like stars. Then Hal had told him of his decision to run for sheriff. "Even though we may have title to our land again, we can't claim it," Hal explained. "Not as long as Cleary sits in his office. He'd just find ways to take it back. Or frame us on some charge, and make sure we get shot 'escaping.' It'd be the same for most of the other people who can claim their land now. I've been talking to a few of them over the past few days. We all agree that someone has to run against Cleary. I guess that somebody'll be me."

Hal told Gabe that he'd been holding back, waiting to see if the raid on the county records would be successful. "The word'll go out now," Hal told him. "There'll be men riding in here in the morning. Armed men. We'll head into town, and I'll file."

Gabe had nodded. Hal and the other men, those victimized by Cleary, were now beginning to do what they should have done long ago. Band together to defeat their enemy. If they did not have the courage to defend their land, they should have stayed in the Eastern cities, where citizens were taught to let others protect them. As if that could be done, as if corruption and greed would not eventually turn the protectors against them.

That was when he had decided to go back to the valley. Even if he had been acting in defense of greater rights, he had been breaking many laws, he'd killed lawmen. It would not do to let everyone see how closely Hal was connected to him.

So he prepared to ride out. As he'd saddled his horse, Becky had come up to him. "You're going away," she said sadly.

He reached down to caress her cheek. "I'll be back. I won't be far away."

She looked down at the ground. "But someday . . . you'll go away forever."

It was not a question. Gabe studied the girl's somber face. He saw that there were tears in her eyes, but they were not tears of desperation, but rather, tears of a transient sadness. How young she is, he thought. Therefore, how resilient. "Yes," he finally said. "Someday I will ride away from here. That is my nature."

He'd left her, then, left them all, but before he'd ridden out of the yard he'd promised Hal he would be back to keep an eye on the election. So far, it was a promise he had not kept. A strange lethargy held him in the valley.

He considered the idea of staying here through the summer and fall, until the cold weather began, enjoying the silence, the beauty of the place. Then, on to California, to see the place where there was no winter.

And now, this uneasiness. It had been growing over the past two days. He could not quite put his finger on what it was, but he found himself studying the landscape around him with nervous attention. It was a feeling he could not shake off. Something had disturbed the peace of his little valley.

When he got up on the morning of the third day, the uneasiness had reached a peak he could no longer ignore. For reasons he could not have explained he decided to forego his usual dress of breechclout and moccasins. Instead, he dressed in his traveling clothes. He even went so far as to pack most of his gear in his saddlebags, and to roll up his bedroll.

He ate some dried deer meat, and considered his plan for making pemmican. He had gone so far as to stand up and approach the drying racks when, suddenly, all of his senses leaped to full alertness.

He spun to face left, toward the valley's entrance. A flock of crows had flown into the air from the place where they normally nested, a tall, dead old tree. He listened to their angry cries, then became aware of a stillness all around him. The animals and birds that lived near his camp had gotten used to him, and he had gotten used to their myriad small daytime noises. Now there was nothing. It was as if all life in the valley had been suspended.

Long Rider exploded into action. His horse was near; he slung his saddle up onto its back, followed by the saddlebags. Both rifles went into their saddle scabbards. He was putting on his Thunderbird coat when the first of the men broke cover, about three hundred yards away. More men followed as Long Rider leaped into the saddle and pulled his horse's head around. He dug his heels into the animal's flank, urging it into a gallop, heading toward the upper end of the valley.

Five men. He counted five, racing toward him. The first shot sounded. A bullet spanged off a tree trunk to his right. Long Rider leaned forward, lying close to his horse's neck, urging him on. His lead was down to about two hundred fifty yards; the men were coming on fast. But now the great speed of Long Rider's mount began to show; it was also fresh, and his pursuers must be riding tired animals. He began to lengthen his lead, until it was back to three hundred yards.

The valley narrowed quickly, its width dwindling as cliffs began to close in from the sides. Ahead lay a narrow entrance between stone ramparts. Long Rider pounded in through this entrance, then stopped. He looked about him frantically. Where was it?

Then he saw the rope, dangling down a ledge of rock. The wind must have moved it. He rode his horse ahead a dozen yards, then ran back on foot toward the rope.

His pursuers were much closer now. He could make out their features. More shots rang out, some coming quite close.

Long Rider scrambled up onto a small ledge so that he could reach the rope. He seized it, then swung all his weight on it. For a minute, nothing happened. Then, above him, something gave, and the rope suddenly became slack in his hands.

He had to get out of here. He slid down from the ledge and ran for his horse. Behind him, a low rumbling sound began. Two days earlier, when the uneasiness had begun, he'd carefully reconnoitered his surroundings. Discovering the narrow upper entrance to the valley, he'd spent an entire day up on its slopes, undermining a big ledge of rock and debris that had been washed loose by winter rains. He'd wedged a small log under what he considered the key rock holding all the rest in place, then tied the end of his spare rope to the end of the log, turning it into a crude lever.

Now the log came loose, and so did the rocks and debris above it. The first of the pursuers had almost reached the narrow entranceway when several tons of rocks came thundering down. The man pulled his horse back at the last moment, narrowly escaping being buried alive.

The dust was still settling when Long Rider reached

his horse and remounted. He studied the pile of debris behind him, finally satisfying himself that the way out of the valley was satisfactorily blocked. He rode away up a narrow gorge, knowing that he'd gained time.

But only time. He'd sensed, from the way that they'd attacked, that these men were not about to give up. There had been something remorseless about their charge.

Long Rider rode for half an hour. The gorge rose higher and higher, until it opened out onto a small plateau. Then he began to double back. Half a mile farther along the plateau became a narrow ledge that overlooked the valley. Dismounting, he took his binoculars and moved to the edge of the ledge.

They were still in the valley, moving around his lean-to and sweat lodge. He counted five men. Four of them were wearing long light-colored coats, and big hats. He studied them through his binoculars. Those four men also wore big, almost identical mustaches that drooped down past the corners of their mouths. He could not make out their eyes at this distance, but he had no doubt they would be hard eyes. The eyes of professional manhunters. Hard men who would go after anyone they were paid to hunt down. Long Rider had little doubt who had sent these men. Cleary and Duval appeared to have upped the ante.

But it was the fifth man who worried Long Rider the most. He was an Indian. It was difficult to tell his tribe because he was mostly dressed in cast-off white man's clothing, except for moccasins and a beaded belt. His hair was long and black, hanging down over his shoulders. He was moving around the camp, examining everything, probably puzzled by the sweat lodge, wondering what kind of man he had been hired to track.

Which would not keep him from doing his job. He was the one to fear, the tracker, the bloodhound, who would hunt down his quarry even if it took him a year. And Long Rider had little doubt that the four white men were also the kind who would stay on his trail until he was dead.

Unless he killed them first. He considered going back to his horse for the Sharps. The range was long, and he'd be shooting downward, but maybe he could hit one, maybe even two of the men before they ran for cover. But just at that moment, as if he'd read Long Rider's mind, the Indian looked up and saw him. Maybe light had flashed off the lenses of the binoculars. Or maybe the Indian was just that good.

The Indian pointed. Below, binoculars were raised to eye level. Two of the white men walked over to their horses. Long Rider watched them pull long, heavy rifles from saddle scabbards. Long Rider raised his binoculars again. The rifles had tubes about two feet long fastened above the barrels. He'd heard about those tubes. Rifle telescopes.

The two men rested their rifles on the saddles of their horses. Both rifles fired at about the same time; Long Rider could see white puffs of smoke blossom from the muzzles.

Fortunately, he ducked. One of the bullets nicked the crown of his hat, right where his forehead had been a moment before. Incredible shooting.

Long Rider backed away from the edge of the bluff before the men could fire again. He slithered along on his belly until he found a bush to hide behind. Once again he looked down into the valley. The men still had their rifles to their shoulders. They seemed to be scanning the ledge top through their telescopes. One of the rifles stopped moving, seemed to be aimed right at Long Rider. He rolled away, and a second later a bullet whistled past where he had been.

It was time to ride. They'd eventually find a way up here, and if they trapped him in the open, they'd kill him with those amazingly accurate rifles. But before heading for his horse, Long Rider risked one more look over the edge.

The rifles were no longer aimed in his direction. All five men were mounting their horses. They seemed to be heading toward the upper entrance to the valley. But why would they do that? It was hopelessly blocked. It would take them a day or two to dig away the debris.

One man reached behind him, into his saddlebags. Long Rider saw him take out several cylindrical objects.

The man selected two of the objects, then put the rest back into his saddlebags.

Dynamite. They were going to blast their way through. Now it was indeed time to ride.

He'd gone only about a mile when he heard the blast. He'd have to assume they'd gotten through. They'd be on his trail in no time . . . especially with the Indian doing the tracking. And if they caught him in the open . . .

He would have to make sure they did not.

For the next three hours, Long Rider worked at hiding his trail. But he only worked just hard enough to make it look as if he were trying to hide it. Because he wanted them to follow.

By the middle of the afternoon Long Rider was passing through an area of thick brush and weeds. Visibility was very poor. Now he really began to hide his tracks. He knew he was losing time, but that no longer mattered. If what he had planned did not work, nothing would ever matter for him again.

He quietly led his tired horse into a tangle of thickets, then dismounted. He left everything behind, even his pistols, taking with him only his knife. He wore just trousers and shirt, and he would have dispensed with the shirt if he had not been afraid that light, striking his bare skin, might give him away.

He doubled back on his trail. There was a place, about half a mile back, that might work. He found it, a dense thicket, with a big tree rising above the surrounding tangle of brush. Most of the tree was lost in thick foliage. He crawled up into the tree, then lay along a branch, knife in hand, waiting.

Half an hour passed. Finally, he could hear sounds . . . the white men, talking. He had counted on that, on their impatience. "Where the hell'd that fucking Indian go now?" he heard one of them mutter.

"Looking for sign, Morgan," another man replied. "Hard to track in this jungle."

A muttered reply. Good. Long Rider had counted on that; the Indian scouting wide, looking for sign. He'd have to come this way—Long Rider had left just enough evidence of his passage to attract the Indian.

A slight rustle from farther up the trail. Long Rider lay flat along the limb, trying to blend in with the foliage. He'd expected to hear the soft sound of hooves, but there was only the sibilant shuffle of moccasined feet. The Indian was on foot.

That was bad. Long Rider had climbed up into the tree so that he could leap onto a man riding a horse. Now the drop would be much greater. But he'd have to do it. The Indian was in sight now, gliding along the path, his obsidian eyes darting right and left, toward the edges of the trail. The Indian knew this was a good place for an ambush, and he was proceeding cautiously.

Long Rider waited until the Indian was right below him, then he launched himself from the limb. But his shirt caught on a small spiky branch. It did not slow him, but as he started to drop, the shirt tore. The sound was small, but enough to alert the Indian below.

The Indian twisted to the side, almost avoiding Long Rider's falling body entirely. Long Rider's left arm slammed into the man's neck, staggering him, but the Indian continued to twist away, just barely evading the slashing blade of Long Rider's knife.

The fall had slightly stunned Long Rider. He'd hit feet first, his fall partly broken by the Indian, but he staggered and went down, rolling immediately, coming to his feet as a continuation of the roll.

He expected to hear a shot, but then realized he had not seen a weapon on the Indian when he'd spotted him coming down the trail. Except for a knife. And that knife was now in the Indian's hand as he launched himself at Long Rider.

Long Rider leaped to the side, tried to grab the knife arm, but missed. The Indian's knife point sliced a shallow cut in Long Rider's left forearm.

The two men now stood facing one another, a yard apart. It had gone badly. Long Rider expected to hear the Indian call out, bringing the other men down on him. But the man remained silent, his dark, expressionless eyes fastened on Long Rider as the two men circled one another.

Then Long Rider understood. From that one overheard

snatch of conversation among the white hunters, he could imagine their general contempt for the Indian, simply because he was an Indian. The Indian would have a matching contempt for them, he would want to finish this for himself, he would want to show those arrogant white men that he, and he alone, was all that was needed to bring in the man they were after.

Which turned out to be the Indian's death warrant. Long Rider lunged, slashed, missed as the Indian danced back out of the way. Then Long Rider appeared to slip, going down onto his left hand to regain his balance, and now the Indian charged, knife thrusting toward Long Rider's neck.

But Long Rider had not slipped. It had been a feint, and as he straightened, he threw the handful of dirt he had scooped up straight into the Indian's face. It was not much of a diversion, but proved enough to distract the other man just long enough for Long Rider to slip past the Indian's guard, and drive the knife deep into his chest.

The Indian stiffened, his mouth falling open. Long Rider seized the other man's knife hand and held him immobile. The Indian seized Long Rider's hand, too, trying to force it away from his chest, so that he could pull the knife out of his body.

But his strength was going fast. Slowly, the Indian's legs buckled. He went down onto his knees, his hand falling away from Long Rider's wrist. Their faces were only inches apart, they were staring straight into one another's eyes. Long Rider saw the light go out of his opponent's eyes, then he fell forward onto his face. Long Rider barely had time to pull his knife free.

The fight had not been without sound. Long Rider heard a shout from the direction of the bounty hunters. They were calling for the Indian. There would be no answer, and he doubted they'd be able to backtrack to where the body lay.

Long Rider slipped away into the brush. Within ten minutes he was back where he had left his horse. He quickly outfitted himself again, then mounted. Now he would play out the rest of this drama. Those rifles with the telescopes would not be worth a damn in this brush.

He looped around in a circle. It was easy enough to find the men; they were making far too much noise. He could hear them talking. "I think the bastard got the Indian," one of them was saying.

There was a short silence. Another man spoke. "Maybe we should fan out, do a search."

"Uh-uh. In brush like this, he'd just pick us off one by one. Hell, if he could get that Indian . . . We'd better stay together, ride out of here until we find someplace where we can see more than a few feet. Then we'll figure another way to go after him."

There was a general mutter of agreement. Long Rider could hear them moving through the brush. They would have to pass not too far away.

He rode up onto a small rise, the only one in the area. Through thinning brush he was able to see the trail the men had ridden up earlier, looking for him. Now they were coming back.

He slipped the Sharps from its scabbard. He was counting on one thing, and one thing alone to end this quickly. If he was wrong . . .

The men came into view, riding along the trail two abreast. He tried to pick out the man he wanted, but had trouble recognizing him at first, and when he did, he saw that the man was partially screened by the man riding alongside him. He had to make them separate a little.

He cocked the rifle. The loud *clunck-click* of the big hammer going back was enough to attract the men's attention. "There he is!" one shouted.

They were all reaching for rifles. But as their horses milled about, Long Rider saw his chance. He raised the Sharps and aimed—straight at the saddlebags of the man who had the dynamite.

Long Rider fired. The heavy slug slammed straight into the saddlebags, knocking the man's horse sideways, although there was no time for it to fall, because the dynamite went off with a thunderous roar. Brush was shredded, and so was flesh. Horses and men were blown to pieces, so that when Long Rider rode closer, under a rain of dirt and pieces of horse, man, and equipment, he saw that only one of the men who'd come hunting for him was still alive, a wreck of a man, lying on the ground several yards from where the explosion had occurred, missing one arm, with his face hanging in shreds. He heard Long Rider approach, and looked up, out of his single remaining eye. He croaked something from a ruined throat. Perhaps it was a plea.

Long Rider shot him through the heart. The man fell back, dead. Long Rider quickly surveyed the scene. Two horses remained alive. He shot both of them through the head.

Then he turned away from the carnage and urged his horse down the trail. He had an impression of time slipping by. Cleary and Duval had sent these men after him. Obviously they considered it important that he be disposed of. Considering the quality of the men they'd sent, they would probably figure that he was already as good as dead. And if they placed so much importance on getting him out of the way, they must be planning some much larger move.

Long Rider pressed his horse onward, as quickly as the big black could go. Hal was in danger. He could sense it.

CHAPTER NINETEEN

Long Rider pushed his horse harder than he should have, but the big stallion responded well. By late afternoon he was approaching the Jackson place. Immediately his instincts told him that something was wrong. Perhaps it was the absence of the slight tang of wood smoke from Mary's perpetually burning cook stove. Or perhaps just the absence of a sense of any life itself.

The house was empty. Long Rider was sure of it as he cautiously rode closer. At least, empty of anything living. His eyes searched the surrounding terrain, looking for ambushes. He could detect nothing. Birds hopped about in the trees in total unconcern. A raccoon loped by the house, obviously at ease, until it spotted Long Rider. Then it stopped dead in its tracks and hunched, head down, while it studied him. Having reached a decision, it quickly scuttled into the brush.

Taking the Winchester, Long Rider got down from his horse and walked up onto the porch. The old boards squealed under his weight. Hal had bragged about those miserable boards, claiming that they were the best warning possible against intruders. Long Rider had agreed . . . except that he was now the intruder.

The front door was slightly ajar. He pushed it open all the way with the muzzle of his rifle. He waited a moment, listening for sounds, perhaps someone inside trying to settle into a better position. Or the cocking of a weapon.

Nothing. The place had a flat, empty feeling of desertion. He strode inside and quickly checked the rooms. No one was there. Hal, and Mary, and Becky, were gone.

But so were their clothes. And the kitchen pots and pans, the dishes, even the small tools that make it possible to live in a house. Everything was gone, lock, stock, and barrel. But, had they left on their own, or by coercion?

Long Rider walked back outside. There were no horses in the corral. He'd noticed that right away. He checked the barn. The old wagon was missing, too. Now he noticed its tracks leaving the yard. They'd cut deep into the ground. The wagon had been heavily loaded.

It was not difficult to follow the wagon tracks. They soon joined the main road that led down out of the mountains. Long Rider rode along quickly, scanning to the sides to see if there was any sign of the wagon leaving the road.

There was not, until he reached the flats, about ten miles farther along. There the wheel ruts turned off the main road, cutting to the right, over open land. Once again it was a trail very easy to follow.

It was almost dark by the time he saw the buildings ahead, a big adobe house, with barns and corrals. Other outbuildings radiated outward from the main house. He moved in slowly, using every bit of cover he could find. The wagon was sitting in front of the house. It appeared to be empty.

But the house was not. In the growing dusk, light beamed from several windows. Long Rider saw men moving around the yard, between buildings that looked like bunkhouses and cook shacks. Perhaps the Jacksons had been abducted by Cleary, and were being held here.

Then he saw a slim figure leave the house and walk toward the wagon. At first he thought it was a boy, then realized that it was Becky. She leaned into the wagon and picked up something. It looked like a large pot. She turned and walked back into the house.

She did not walk like a person being held captive. And then Long Rider realized what had happened. Hal, and Mary and Becky, having recovered title to their ranch, had simply moved back home.

Gabe rode straight into the yard. One of the men over by the bunkhouse saw him when he was still a hundred yards away. "Hey!" he shouted. "Hey . . . it's him!"

Several men came out of the bunkhouse and stood watching him approach. Hal must have heard the commotion. He came out of the house carrying a rifle. "Thank God!" he burst out when he saw Gabe. "We thought you were dead."

Gabe swung down from his horse. "Not that I've noticed. What made you think that?"

Hal sighed. "Cleary and Duval. They've been noising it around that a bunch of bounty hunters were after your hide. That they would be back in a day or two with your body. They were so cocksure that . . . well, some of us started to believe it."

Gabe stood holding the reins of his horse. "I'm not that easy to kill," he said matter-of-factly.

"Maybe. But we know they're out hunting you. Some of our people saw them riding into town. A hard-looking bunch, from what I hear."

"As hard as they come."

Hal's eyebrows raised. "You've seen them?"

"Uh-huh."

A small crowd had gathered. Gabe saw Mary standing on the big veranda that ran all the way around the adobe. Becky had her head stuck out of a window, her face alight as she saw Gabe. Half a dozen men were standing about fifteen feet away, listening.

"You gave them the slip, then," Hal said.

"In a manner of speaking."

Hal became all business. "I suppose we better put out extra guards. From what I hear, they're cocky enough to ride right in here after you. They . . . "

Then something about Gabe's manner got through to Hal. "Oh," he murmured. "I understand now. Guess they won't be coming after anyone."

"No," Gabe said quietly. "They're dead."

"Jesus," one of the men said half under his breath. "I seen those bastards. Turned my blood cold. Real killers. An' he got 'em all."

Gabe glanced toward the house. He'd expected Becky to come running outside to greet him, but she was still leaning out of the window. Hal saw where he was looking. "Come inside," he said. "We've got a lot of talking to do."

But Gabe took care of his horse first, unsaddling the tired animal. He removed the bit and reins and replaced them with a soft, pliant hackamore made out of woven horsehair. It would give the animal freedom to eat without the bother of a bit, and at the same time make it easy to catch him later. He turned the horse into one of the corrals. A man ran up to take his horse gear to the tack room. Only then did Gabe start toward the house, carrying his saddlebags and rifles.

Mary gave him a big hug as soon as he stepped up onto the veranda. He saw Becky inside. She was smiling, with her hands clasped together, but she made no move toward him until he was inside, then she flew into his arms and gave him a big smacking kiss, on the cheek. He hesitated, his arms still around her. She seemed subtly different, as if she were holding something back. It must be the new place, he thought. And all the people around. She was a little bashful. Funny . . . bashfulness didn't seem like Becky. But her body in his arms definitely seemed like Becky, solid, warm, pliant. Maybe later . . .

Hal urged him toward the living room. "Mary'll rustle up some chow," he said. "We have to talk."

It was a big room, with heavy furniture. Like most adobes, the walls were not perfectly flat, but curved irregularly, with rounded corners. The walls were also very thick, nearly three feet. The floor was of polished tile, with occasional thick carpets. A huge oak table, well-polished, stood near one wall. Definitely a step up from the shack where the Jacksons had nursed him back to health. Gabe could understand better, now, the Jacksons' bitterness over losing their property. The house was big, handsome, comfortable, the buildings outside were the right ones for running the place, and most of all, the land Gabe had ridden over to get here was beautiful, rich. Fine land for raising cattle and horses.

Hal seemed different. More confident, poised. And more harried. "Pardon all the hoopla out there," he said. "But Cleary's been putting out the word that you were a goner. Did it to pry men away from me. You've become kind of a symbol around here, you know. The one man who was able to stand up to Cleary and Duval and make them bleed. With you gone, people might start thinking again that neither of those bastards can be beat. They would start to drift away, and then Cleary would have a clear shot at getting rid of me for good."

Gabe nodded. People who had let a man like Cleary dominate them in the first place would be easily discouraged by any setbacks. "The campaign for sheriff," he asked Hal. "How's it going?"

Hal ran a hand through his hair. He definitely was under tension. "Well enough. In general, most of the people around here hate Cleary's guts. Duval's, too. But they'll only back someone who looks like a winner. That's Cleary's strategy . . . to make me look like a loser. If he can isolate me . . . "

Gabe took a closer look at Hal. Under the tension, he thought he could detect a fierce energy. "You like this, don't you? Running for office, being at the center of things."

Hal grinned. "Yeah. Makes me feel alive."

His grin faded. "Now . . . let's plan."

He quickly brought Gabe up to date on what had been happening. Cleary and Duval, opening their purse strings, had been bringing hardcase gunmen into the area. "A little more than a dozen, so far," Hal said. "Not counting the ones he sent after you. And I don't know how well these people I'm working with will stand up to hired guns. Most of my people aren't killers by nature. They're wavering. Especially after the rumor about you being dead. Now . . . with you back . . . "

"Yes. Now you have a man who's a killer by nature," Gabe said quietly.

Hal flushed. "I didn't mean it that way."

"Don't apologize. You've decided to become a leader. And a leader, a man with responsibility for others, has to think differently."

Privately, Gabe preferred the Hal he'd known before. He remembered the saying he'd read: "Power corrupts. Absolute power corrupts absolutely." Saddest of all, the power many men looked for had no meaning at all. The only power that mattered was the power that a man had over himself. That was why, among the People, there were no chiefs in the way the white men thought of a chief. Nothing like a king. Leaders among the People were simply those whom others admired enough to follow. Once admiration for them faded, so did any influence they might have. There were few men more independent than a Lakota warrior. Which, Gabe reflected sadly, was one of the reasons they'd been beaten by the white men, who were willing to submit themselves to the will of others. To discipline.

Which was what needed to be reestablished here. "Tell me where these men of Cleary's are," he said. "It's time they learn what it is to feel fear."

As they rode, Gabe could not keep himself from casting surreptitious glances at one of the men riding along with him. There were four of them, but this particular man, a man in his late twenties, good-looking, quiet, was the one who interested him the most.

It was all because of the way Becky had been looking at him. His name was Jonathan. Gabe had at first been confused by Becky's nervousness, but when he caught the quick, warm looks she was casting in Jonathan's direction, he understood. Obviously Hal had not been the only one changed by their new circumstances. Or rather, the return of the old ones. He had to remind himself that the girl was only looking out for herself. He'd as good as told her, just a few days earlier, that soon, he'd be riding away. Alone.

And now, along comes Jonathan. A fine-looking man. And he was in the act of reclaiming his father's land, a big ranch about twenty miles away. Cleary had cheated

Jonathan's father out of the land, then killed him when he came after him to get it back. Now it was the son's turn to try.

Jonathan had been one of the men Gabe had picked to accompany him, partly because he obviously had plenty of reason to want to fight hard against Cleary. And there would definitely be fighting. Hal had told Gabe that half a dozen of Cleary's hired guns were holed up at a line camp about ten miles away. Gabe had decided to move against them. "We'll cut down their numbers," he'd told Hal. "And teach the rest to fear us, the way Cleary and Duval want us to fear them."

Becky had been standing on the veranda to see them off, Gabe, and Jonathan, and the three other men. Damned if she hadn't been wearing a dress. She'd looked lovely. Amazingly lovely. He'd noticed how she kept glancing from Jonathan to himself and back to Jonathan. Indecision was written all over the girl's face, but Jonathan had not seemed to notice it. He'd beamed at the girl happily, obviously totally and insanely in love.

Gabe snatched himself away from his reverie. They were nearing the line camp. It would be stupid to get killed because his mind was on a girl.

They stopped their horses behind a small rise. Gabe chose Jonathan to walk to the top with him. He bristled a little at the other man's proximity, but he wanted to study him. He'd had a brief thought of sending him into the thick of the fight. Maybe he'd get killed. Then he'd felt ashamed of himself. He remembered the story in his mother's Bible, the part about the Jewish king who'd sent the husband of a woman he coveted to certain death. That was a coward's move.

The line camp lay below, a lone shack, with a corral nearby. Smoke rose from the shack's single chimney. Three men sat outside on rickety chairs, passing a bottle. Movement inside suggested others, probably no more than two or three, considering the shack's size. Horses, already saddled, stood in the corral.

Gabe and Jonathan walked back down the hill toward the others. As they mounted, Jonathan asked, "How are you gonna handle this?"

Gabe thought about it for a moment. "Ride straight in," he finally said. "Kill them."

The other men looked surprised. Gabe did not wait for objections, but rode for the top of the hill. The others followed. When they reached it, he turned to them. "You stay here . . . give me covering fire. Make them keep their heads down."

By now the three men below, sitting outside the shack, had seen the five horsemen up on the hilltop. One stood up, called something toward the shack. Three more men came outside, two carrying rifles.

Time to attack, now, before they could organize a defense. Gabe pulled out the big Sharps, then sighted on one of the men with a rifle. *Kablam!* The big slug took the man in the chest. He went flying backward, crashing against the wall of the shack.

Gabe immediately returned the Sharps to its scabbard, then pulled out the Winchester. Digging his heels into his horse's side, he charged over the lip of the hill, straight down toward the men below.

Gabe was full of anger. He knew it, he could feel it. The anger was partly against the men he was charging. Men who killed for money. Killed good people if the pay was high enough. He knew that he was also angry at himself, angry at letting himself get trapped in an emotional box. Over Becky. A girl. But what a girl!

He began swerving his horse from side to side. Three of the men had opened fire. Bullets buzzed around him. Then he heard answering fire from the men he'd left up on the hill. One of the men below went down.

Gabe stood upright in the stirrups, firing. He saw another man stagger. Gabe let out a loud war cry and continued firing. Bullets, his own, and the bullets of the men behind him, were tearing up dirt all around the gunmen. Propping up the one Gabe had wounded, they ran toward the door of the shack. Gabe was close now. One of the men turned and pointed a pistol at him. Gabe shot him through the neck with his rifle. The man dropped his pistol, grabbed his neck, which was spurting blood, and fell to the ground, where he proceeded to choke to death.

Gabe barely noticed him. A cold killing anger still seethed within him. For weeks he'd suffered at the hands of men Cleary and Duval had bought for money. Mercenaries. He continued riding straight on in, but the men were all in the house now. No more easy targets. And a rifle barrel was pointing out of the doorway, aimed at him.

He swung his horse to the left, toward the building's side wall, away from the door. The man in the doorway fired, but missed. The bullet zipped by so close to Gabe's ear that he could feel the heat of its passage.

Then he was swinging down from his horse. There was a window in that side wall. If he could get to it before the men inside the shack had the presence of mind to cover it . . .

It was going to be close. He was against the side wall now, but could still hear firing from the front door. He turned, and now he could see why. Jonathan, realizing what he was trying to do, had also charged, straight at the door, weaving his horse the way Gabe had done, firing his Winchester. Gabe stopped for just a moment to admire the other man's courage. It took guts to charge straight in against a barricaded foe.

Then, so he would not waste the other man's bravery, Gabe leaped toward the window. No one there yet; they were all concentrated against Jonathan. Gabe thrust the barrel of his rifle inside. Dim, shadowy shapes. He opened fire. A man screamed, then went down. Another tried to turn, to bring his rifle around. Gabe shot him. The last survivor, terrified, ran out the front door. Gabe heard a fusillade of shots. Then . . . moaning.

He raced around to the front. The other three men were now riding in hard from the hill. Gabe looked around quickly. He saw Jonathan's horse standing nearby. The saddle was empty.

Then he saw Jonathan. He was about five yards away, still on his feet. Holding his rifle in one hand, he walked slowly toward one of the bodies lying in front of the shack. Gabe saw that he had his other hand pressed against his side. Blood showed.

"Hit bad?" Gabe asked.

Jonathan shook his head. "I think it bounced off a rib. Just as I shot this one."

He pointed down at the man lying at his feet. The man groaned. He was still alive.

Gabe quickly checked him for hidden weapons, then rolled him over. He was shot through the stomach. Gabe doubted he'd live another ten minutes.

The man seemed to come to the same conclusion. "God," he moaned. "It wasn't s'posed to work out this way. You was s'posed to . . ."

Alarm flared inside Gabe. "Supposed to what?" he demanded.

Now the man focused on Gabe. His eyes widened in surprise. "You!" he burst out. "They told us you was dead. It was gonna be so easy. . . ."

"Easy to do what?" Gabe asked. He wanted to shake the man, make him talk more quickly, but any sudden movement might kill him.

The man coughed up blood. He watched it soaking into his shirtfront, above the big hole in his stomach. "Cleary an' Duval are gonna hit Jackson's house this mornin'. They're gonna do a lot of shootin', then make like they're runnin' away. Then, when Jackson and his men follow, we're s'posed to ride in from the side, ambush 'em, wipe 'em out. We was gonna leave in a few minutes. Good plan . . . but then you hit us here first. . . ."

The man coughed. The sudden movement sent a spasm of agony rippling through his body. "Jesus!" he screamed. Then died.

He was the last one left alive. Gabe leaped to his feet. "You heard what he said. There may be an attack underway at the house. Right now. Let's ride."

They all leaped into their saddles. As they pounded back over the top of the hill, leaving the dead gunmen behind, Gabe pulled his horse close to Jonathan's. "Thanks," he said.

Jonathan nodded. His hand was still pressed to his side, but the bleeding seemed to have stopped.

Then Gabe let the big black's speed pull him ahead of the others. He hated to admit it, but it looked like Becky might have found herself a good man.

CHAPTER TWENTY

The house was definitely under attack; they could hear the firing when they were still a couple of miles away. The temptation was to ride straight on in and help, but Gabe curbed the others. "No . . . let's take a look first."

The fact that there was so much firing argued that the defenders were still quite able to give a good account of themselves. He noticed the pinched, worried look on Jonathan's face as they rode cautiously toward the back of a hill that overlooked the house. Worrying about Becky, no doubt. As he himself was.

From behind a thick stand of bushes they were able to see the fighting below. Hal and the others must have had enough warning; it seemed like everyone had made it inside the house except one man, whose body lay not far from the front door. Numerous puffs of smoke erupted from various windows. The house, with its thick walls, was a natural fortress. Of course, it was also a trap, if an attacking force chose to settle in for a long siege.

But Gabe knew that was not Cleary's plan. He studied the scene below. Cleary had at least a dozen men outside the house, sheltering behind outbuildings and watering troughs. Spread out like that, it would be hard for Gabe and his little force of four to accomplish much if they rode straight in. They could end up surrounded by

Cleary's nicely dispersed group.

The thing to do was get them all together. Gabe was beginning to get the first glimmerings of an idea. Perhaps they could use Cleary's own plan against him.

How was Cleary supposed to know when his own flanking force arrived? Probably some kind of signal. Gabe reached behind him and took a shirt out of his saddlebags. His last clean one. He tied the arms to his rifle barrel, then started to move toward the edge of the hill, where he could be seen by Cleary, but not by the people inside the house.

Then he stopped himself, cursing at his own stupidity. He still had on the buffalo hide coat. He'd be recognized immediately. He handed the crude flag to one of the other men. "Go up there and wave this."

Grinning, realizing what Gabe was doing, as did the other three, the man rode to the edge of the hill and began to wave the shirt. After a few seconds, Gabe saw an answering wave from below, a very surreptitious wave.

Cleary's men, on a prearranged signal, made a concerted rush away from the house, toward a gully where their horses were being held, about two hundred yards away. Sure enough, there was a whoop from the house, and already two or three men were running outside, firing after the retreating enemy. If they were inexperienced enough—and most of the men with Hal had little actual fighting experience—they would let themselves get strung out, far from cover, and then, when Cleary's flanking force rode in, they'd be cut off from the house.

Except that it was not Cleary's flanking force that was waiting behind the hill. Gabe let Cleary's men get all nice and bunched up, then he waved a hand in a signal to attack. He and the four others with him charged down the hill straight at the sheriff's men.

Four of Cleary's hired killers went down in the first volley. For several seconds, Cleary's men were too surprised to fire back. Perhaps they thought that it must be a terrible mistake, that their own relievers had mistakenly opened fire on the wrong people.

Then Gabe's Thunderbird coat and his big black stal-

lion were recognized, and the men below realized they
were trapped. By now the last of the defenders had sallied from the house and were pouring a withering fire
into the backs of the retreating attackers.

Some of Cleary's crowd began throwing down their
weapons. Some were too late, and went down, riddled
with bullets. But there was one man among them, a big
man, who refused to surrender. Gabe saw that it was
Cleary. Roaring with rage, like a wounded bull, Cleary
charged the men who'd sallied from the house. Gabe
saw his rifle blossom smoke one time, and a man fell.
Then the rifle appeared to be empty. Gabe saw Cleary
throw it away in disgust.

Cleary reached for his pistol just as Gabe was sliding
the Sharps from its saddle scabbard. Then a voice cut
through the decreasing sound of firing. An angry voice.
"Cleary!"

It was Hal. He was running toward Cleary, a shotgun
held high. Cleary recognized Hal, and spun to face him.
"You son of a bitch!" Cleary screamed.

The pistol rose. Hal continued to run toward Cleary,
wanting to get within easy shotgun range. Gabe raised
the Sharps, then remembered he'd forgotten to reload
it after the fight at the shack. He was fumbling for a
cartridge when the sharp report of a rifle sounded from
the house.

The bullet's impact spun Cleary halfway around. Gabe
saw a figure standing on the veranda. A figure in skirts.
Mary. She was levering another round into the chamber
when Cleary started to point the pistol toward her.

"Not her, Cleary," Hal shouted. "Me, you bastard."

Cleary started to turn again, but the shotgun roared
before he could get his pistol up. The shot took him in
the stomach, doubling him up. He staggered backward,
clutching his gut, but he still had the pistol in his hand.
He was trying to straighten, to bring the muzzle to
bear . . .

He was hit from each side, through the neck by Mary's
rifle, and in the chest by the load from the barrel of Hal's
shotgun. Blown half in two, he flew backward, then fell
flat on his back. After he hit the ground, he twitched a

few times, then lay still. Gabe could hear Mary's shrill, contemptuous cry, "Steal *our* land, you bastard . . . "

Gabe heard a cry from behind him. He turned. Jonathan was pointing. "Duval," he said. "He made it to the horses."

Sure enough, a thin figure in a dark coat had clambered up onto the back of one of the horses from the gully. Spurring hard, he rode away, coattails flapping.

With Duval riding straight away from him, it was an easy shot for Gabe. No need to lead him at all. Gabe had reloaded the Sharps. Sitting his horse quietly, he sighted in on Duval's back. Strange, he'd never met the man, but he'd been trying to kill Gabe for weeks. Gabe had no doubt it was Duval behind the plan to wipe out Hal. Cleary had been too bull-like to use any subtlety. A dangerous man, Duval. A danger that had to end.

The rifle roared. It took the huge bullet nearly a second to reach Duval, but reach him it did, slamming into his back and launching him over his horse's neck. Immediately several men raced to where he'd fallen. Gabe reloaded the rifle and put it away. He was sure Duval was dead.

He looked around him at the battlefield. Those of Cleary's men who'd survived were being herded together. It was over. The last of his enemies were now dead.

But what about his friends? What about those who'd rallied to him when he was a hunted, wounded man? Hal was walking toward him. Mary was still on the porch, leaning on her rifle. Truly a warrior woman. Hal was a lucky man.

And Becky. She was on the veranda now. He saw that she was holding a rifle, too. But a warrior woman? Not in the same way as Mary. There was greater softness there.

He saw she was looking at him. He rode straight to her, stopping just short of the veranda. She watched him all the way, except for once, when she looked over his shoulder, her eyes studying, appraising.

"He's a good man," Gabe said, knowing she'd been looking at Jonathan. "Brave, steady. He'd make a good husband."

"And you?" she asked, her eyes huge with confusion. "What about you, Gabe? You're going to ride away, aren't you. Just ride right on out of my life."

He nodded. "I think it's time. I've disturbed your life enough."

She stamped her foot in irritation. "Oh, you idiot. You haven't disturbed my life at all. You've made it . . . so much more than it was before. Just say the word, Gabe, and I'll ride away with you."

He slowly shook his head. "I don't live in your kind of world, Becky. Your world is here. With this land. With its people."

She lowered her eyes and nodded slowly. He could see her lips moving, but could not hear the words. He turned his horse. "I'll never forget you," she called softly after him. He turned in the saddle. He was grinning now. His eyes roamed over her body, boldly, with obvious intent. "Me neither."

She blushed as he turned away. He rode over toward the men. Hal was supervising the rounding up of the prisoners. He looked up when he saw Gabe. "Guess this means I win the election," he said, grinning.

"Sure does, Sheriff."

Then Hal noticed the expression on Gabe's face. Hal stopped smiling. "You're leaving."

Gabe nodded. Hal shook his head vehemently. "I'll be sheriff soon enough. I need a good deputy. I . . ."

He stopped talking when he saw the amused smile on Gabe's face. He grinned sheepishly. "I guess I sound kinda foolish, don't I? You're not the kind of man who'd want to be tied down."

Hal could not keep from glancing in Becky's direction. She stood on the veranda, forlorn. Then both Hal and Gabe saw that Jonathan was walking toward her. They noticed animation returning to her face. "It's better for her," Gabe said.

Hal nodded. He turned back to face Gabe. "Jonathan told me how you handled the fighting over at the line shack. And the way you bushwhacked Cleary. He wanted to know if you'd had any military training."

Gabe nodded. "Yes . . . I did. I fought for years under a great general."

"Oh? Which one?"

Now Gabe smiled. "Crazy Horse."

Hal was still looking surprised when Gabe spoke again. "Say good-bye to Mary for me."

Then he turned his horse and rode away.

A special offer for people who enjoy reading the best Westerns published today. If you enjoyed this book, subscribe now and get . . .

TWO FREE

A $5.90 VALUE—NO OBLIGATION

If you enjoyed this book and would like to read more of the very best Westerns being published today, you'll want to subscribe to True Value's Western Home Subscription Service. If you enjoyed the book you just read and want more of the most exciting, adventurous, action packed Westerns, subscribe now.

Each month the editors of True Value will select the 6 very best Westerns from America's leading publishers for special readers like you. You'll be able to preview these new titles as soon as they are published, FREE for ten days with no obligation.

TWO FREE BOOKS

When you subscribe, we'll send you your first month's shipment of the newest and best 6 Westerns for you to preview. With your first shipment, two of these books will be yours as our introductory gift to you absolutely FREE, regardless of what you decide to do. If you like them, as much as we think you will, keep all six books but pay for just 4 at the low subscriber rate of just $2.45 each. If you decide to return them, keep 2 of the titles as our gift. No obligation.

Special Subscriber Savings

When you become a True Value subscriber you'll save money several ways. First, all regular monthly selections will be billed at the low subscriber price of just $2.45 each. That's

WESTERNS!

at least a savings of $3.00 each month below the publishers price. Second, there is never any shipping, handling or other hidden charges—Free home delivery. What's more there is no minimum number of books you must buy, you may return any selection for full credit and you can cancel your subscription at any time. A TRUE VALUE!

Mail the coupon below

To start your subscription and receive 2 FREE WESTERNS, fill out the coupon below and mail it today. We'll send your first shipment which includes 2 FREE BOOKS as soon as we receive it.

Mail To: 557-73428
True Value Home Subscription Services, Inc.
P.O. Box 5235
120 Brighton Road
Clifton, New Jersey 07015-5235

YES! I want to start receiving the very best Westerns being published today. Send me my first shipment of 6 Westerns for me to preview FREE for 10 days. If I decide to keep them, I'll pay for just 4 of the books at the low subscriber price of $2.45 each; a total of $9.80 (a $17.70 value). Then each month I'll receive the 6 newest and best Westerns to preview Free for 10 days. If I'm not satisfied I may return them within 10 days and owe nothing. Otherwise I'll be billed at the special low subscriber rate of $2.45 each; a total of $14.70 (at least a $17.70 value) and save $3.00 off the publishers price. There are never any shipping, handling or other hidden charges. I understand I am under no obligation to purchase any number of books and I can cancel my subscription at any time, no questions asked. In any case the 2 FREE books are mine to keep.

Name _____

Address _____ Apt. # _____

City _____ State _____ Zip _____

Telephone # _____

Signature _____
              (if under 18 parent or guardian must sign)
              Terms and prices subject to change.
Orders subject to acceptance by True Value Home Subscription Services, Inc.